Telling It:
Women and Language Across Cultures

TELLING IT

Women and Language Across Cultures

the transformation of a conference

edited by The Telling It Book Collective:

Sky Lee
Lee Maracle
Daphne Marlatt
Betsy Warland

PRESS GANG PUBLISHERS
VANCOUVER

Canadian Cataloguing in Publication Data

Main entry under title:
Telling it

Includes some material from a conference held Nov. 1988 at Simon Fraser University.
ISBN 0-88974-027-5

1. Canadian literature (English)—Women authors.* 2. Canadian literature (English)—Minority authors.* 3. Canadian literature (English)—20th century.* 4. Canadian literature (English)—20th century—History and criticism.* 5. Women—Literary collections. I. Telling It Book Collective (Vancouver, B.C.)
PS8235.W7T44 1990 C810'.8'09287 C90-091570-6
PR9194.5.W6T44 1990

The five poems by Jeannette Armstrong are from her collection of poetry, *Breath Tracks*, to be published by Williams-Wallace Publishers. Used with permission. "f.) is sure," "mOther muse" and "difference = invisibility," by Betsy Warland, have appeared in *Proper Deafinitions* (Vancouver: Press Gang Publishers, 1990). "mOther muse" originally appeared in *Trois*, vol. 4, no. 1, automne 1988, Montreal. Used with permission.

First Printing October 1990
1 2 3 4 5 93 92 91 90

The Publisher acknowledges financial assistance from the Canada Council.

Editor for the Press: Barbara Kuhne
Design, typesetting and production by Val Speidel
Typeset in Cheltenham ITC at The Typeworks
Printed on acid free paper
Printed and bound in Canada by Friesen Printing

Press Gang Publishers
603 Powell Street
Vancouver, B.C. V6A 1H2 Canada

Contents

Introduction

*Meeting On Fractured Margins**

Daphne Marlatt

photo: LaVerne Harrell Clark

Few conferences live on in their participants' minds as persistently as TELLING IT: WOMEN AND LANGUAGE ACROSS CULTURES has lived in the minds of the four women editing this book. The result of a year-and-a-half of discussion, critique and editing is not so much a proceedings as it is the transformation of a conference, a transformation developed most vividly in Sky Lee's, Lee Maracle's and Betsy Warland's commentaries at the end of this volume. Their commentaries develop issues raised during the two charged days of the TELLING IT conference held in Vancouver, Canada in November 1988. But their commentaries open that discussion into a context that is at once more analytical and more personal.

---

*Editors' note: The texts in this book reflect a decision to respect each author's style of capitalization rather than to impose a standard format.

Analysis of what is closest to us is always difficult: it requires a blend of critical perspective as well as emotional honesty. Each of the women speaking/writing in this book is doing so from inside a personal struggle to articulate what has been painfully felt. Between analysis and pain lies a range of anecdote, morals, humour (both bitter and convivial), story, social critique, and poetry—a blend keyed to the individual life and thought of each writer. The range in this book is remarkable.

The book itself has been in constant process. What began as a proceedings is still traceable as such in PART ONE: *Voices From the Conference*, which highlights the two conference panels, including talks by participating writers, edited transcripts of the ensuing discussion with the audiences and creative writing by seven featured writers. This section also includes one of the three short plays performed at the conference by the women of Vancouver Sath, a Punjabi theatre collective. PART TWO: *Voice(s)-Over*, takes the discussion generated at the conference several steps further. By this point the book *Telling It* has become a passionate analysis of the issues of racism and homophobia, which reflect each other just as they reflect in various and destructive ways on all of us.

Difference is a high-intensity beam. The reflections it raises, both in terms of thought and in terms of images of the self, are painful. To be different in our other-phobic, our alter-(even ultra!)-phobic society is to be branded as somehow less than human: an anguish, an absurdity, a maddening misrepresentation, given the consciousness, the culture, the sheer intelligence speaking in this book.

Each woman has different strategies for countering the dilemma of difference. There is Lee Maracle's lucid analytical fury; Sky Lee's anguished imagery of the "pain of glass"; Joy Kogawa's persistent refusals to be labelled; Betsy Warland's probing wordplays; Jeannette Armstrong's angry and healing vision; Louise Profeit-LeBlanc's ethical wisdom of her people's stories; Barbara Herringer's lesbian straight-talk... to characterize only a few of their strategies.

Native writers Jeannette Armstrong and Lee Maracle articulate their analysis in different ways and with different styles, but their positions are often similar. The emotional generosity of Lee's writing, in both its anger and its work for social change; the visionary power of Jeannette's poetry and her keen sense of cultural difference—these make for passionate critiques. Louise Profeit-LeBlanc's traditional story-telling approach enacts Native tradition and demonstrates the mode of thought Jeannette speaks so eloquently about. Unfortunately, the printed space of a page can't convey the performance quality of Louise's stories with their variety of acting-out sounds and the quiet drama of her voice.

The musing quality of Joy Kogawa's voice, both in her comments and in the excerpt from her novel-in-progress, offers a kind of ethical meditation that pays equal attention to inner needs and outer demands. Sky Lee's humour and acerbic social commentary, on the other hand, sustains a definite individualism even as it insists on a sense of the collective. Both Joy and Sky take aspects of their respective Japanese and Chinese cultures and, as contemporary urban Canadians, transform them to serve their own woman-centred writing purposes.

Betsy Warland and Barbara Herringer, both white lesbian writers, grapple with the issue of their sexual difference within the women's community. In very different ways, each talks about the cultural shift that coming to her lesbianism has meant for her—how profoundly that shift has affected her approach to language and to mainstream culture.

Harjinder Sangra, Jagdish Binning, Anju Hundal and Pindy

Gill, the four women of Vancouver Sath, have written and performed a moving short play about how economic stress on a contemporary Indo-Canadian family ends up victimizing the eldest woman in that family. Their play contributes another voice to the cultural diversity the TELLING IT conference was designed to celebrate.

The Conference Behind the Book

The opportunity to organize TELLING IT: WOMEN AND LANGUAGE ACROSS CULTURES arose in 1988 while i was occupying the Ruth Wynn Woodward Chair of Women's Studies at Simon Fraser University. It was something of an anomaly: a conference organized within an academic structure, but designed as a non-academic, community-focused conference, or rather communities-(in the plural)-focused. Limited in size yet aspiring to showcase the writing and thought of women who are marginalized in different ways, it drew on the three largest groups of marginalized women in British Columbia. So it featured women writers and performers from the Native Indian, Asian-Canadian and lesbian communities in B.C., with one performer from Whitehorse, Yukon and one writer with West Coast roots attending from Toronto.

It was designed to be a celebration of the work by these writers—work which i felt to be ground-breaking in different but related ways—and a space for dialogue between them and their audiences. It was meant to provoke discussion that seemed long overdue about difference on several crucial rift-lines, not the least of which are the rifts of race and sexual orientation. As such, the conference was an attempt at yet another talking-space in a series of attempts to air these rift-lines which have become so apparent in the women's movement.

Bringing women together in the same room implied a hope that our differences were not completely unbridgeable, that women with dissimilar, even unequal experiences of oppression, might be able to speak openly and hear each other openly, might even (and this was a wilder hope) find some sense of shared ground to enable us to help each other in our struggle against the forces of a society that continues to marginalize us. I hesitate to say "us" because of the real differences in experience of oppression of women on the fractured margins of our patriarchal/colonial society. On the other hand, i say "us" because, as a lesbian writer, i had a stake in this conference. Every woman who spoke or performed at that conference had some stake in it, by which i mean some urgency to say where she was coming from and what she knew about the power of language (as both enabling and repressive), the power of writing and story-telling, and how these powers can be tapped in ways that are both spiritually nourishing and politically effective.

So, yes, there was a certain idealism that fueled this conference. But the trouble with idealism (as a number of comments from the audiences bore out) is that it can overlook the pain of real differences in oppression for the sake of some fantasized solidarity. Differences did surface, sometimes in suppressed, even suppressive ways (as you will see from the editors' commentaries), but differences also surfaced in lucid and edifying ways (as you will see from the writers' talks and their comments during discussions with the audiences).

TELLING IT has been criticized for discriminating against some women of colour by not including other communities, but a conference of its size could not have represented more communities without becoming a collection of "token" women. It seemed important to have several women from each marginalized group there—important for the dialogue that might ensue. The three Native writers who were featured at the conference, Jeannette Armstrong, Lee Maracle and Louise Profeit-LeBlanc, together with Native arts activist Viola Thomas, who moderated both panels and introduced each speaker, supported one another in creating an atmosphere that seemed both ceremonial and welcoming. Certain Native Indian courtesies, like thanking the speakers for sharing their thoughts and honouring elders in the audience, were extended to all, regardless of race. Viola's introductions and her panel summaries were consistently warm and generous, and her opening remarks sounded an important theme:

> I think that there has been a notion within this country that lesbian writers, women of colour—whether they're Indigenous women or other ethnic minority writers—there's been a strong notion that there hasn't been recognition, there hasn't been acknowledgement in terms of their efforts in writing. And I think what's important to understand in coming together in a conference like this, is that those stories have always been around, they have never been lost, and today you will hear testimony from these women of their struggles and their experiences in playing an active role in writing.

She also urged the audience to support the writers in very tangible ways:

> I encourage each of you to continue empowering these women and the work that they're doing, and you can do that in many different ways. You can do that by raising the issue within the learning schools of whether or not their books are part of the schooling. You can do that by seeking out their books and reading them. You can do that by sharing what you learned here today with your beloved ones, because each of us in our way can help each other come to a better understanding by really sharing.

These remarks went a long way towards creating a space for listening and speaking that was, if not secure—how could it be, given the emotionally-charged issues of homophobia and racism?—at least open enough to make the uttering of alternate realities and dissenting viewpoints possible.

The Asian-Canadian writers and performers came from

Punjabi, Chinese, and Japanese communities. The two writers who represented the lesbian community were both white, which i now realize contributed to an unfortunate erasure of lesbian women of colour. This was not my intention. White lesbian writers are marginalized within the literary mainstream, but lesbian women of colour are also marginalized there, as women of colour, as well as within their own communities, as lesbians. While this issue surfaced at the conference, it was never fully discussed there.

Although i feel that the TELLING IT conference was a necessary step in an attempt to form a meeting ground on the very fractured margins we inhabit, i would not again presume to organize a conference, even in part, *for* women of colour. The time is overdue for women of colour to have organizing power themselves, though this is difficult to attain with limited means. In Canadian universities, a traditional support-ground for conferences, women of colour are severely under-represented on faculties across the country. Women's Studies programs, which have closer ties than any other departments with the communities outside the academy, need in particular to rectify this situation. But women's conferences can be organized from outside this traditional source of funding. They can be organized within alternative, non-academic formats, with styles that feel comfortable for the community or communities they represent, and at sites that are very different from classroom structures. Women of colour, with varied organizing skills and styles, may well open the way to wholly different kinds of women's conferences than North America has been accustomed to.

Some Events Behind This Conference

The Women and Words/Les femmes et les mots conference held in Vancouver in 1983 was the first conference to bring together women working in literature from various communities across Canada—anglophone and francophone, women of colour and white women. It was the first women's conference in Canada where racism was openly addressed. Two years later an attempt was made to organize a second Women and Words conference in Toronto, but the organizing committee splintered on this exact issue. Then in 1987, women in Montreal got together to take on the arduous task of organizing the Third International Feminist Book Fair, an exciting occasion which brought together women from many different countries in 1988. Again, racism was an issue, with many women of colour in Canada feeling that because there were no women of colour on the organizing committee, the programme of readings and panels reflected a white bias. Despite this, women of colour made their voices heard, most notably in what I believe was the largest group reading ever given by Native women writers from across Canada and the U.S. Women of colour were also heard in workshops and panels investigating such issues as appropriation of Native material, how language reflects identity, empowerment through memory, and the relationship between racism, sexism and patriarchy.

It was at this book fair that Lee Maracle, on behalf of Native writers, asked Anne Cameron to stop using Native culture and sacred stories in her books and to move over and make room for Native writers who are writing out of their own experiences and traditions. Anne publicly agreed that moving over was a necessary step for white writers to take at this crucial point, but Lee's request subsequently caused a storm in the Writers' Union of Canada, where white writers accused Native writers, and other white writers who supported this position, of imposing censorship on the (read, white) imagination. It seems that what white feminists have begun to painfully learn about the extent of our ignorance in our interactions with women of colour is still scandalous news in the (predominantly white) literary mainstream.

At the same time as all this was going on, i was hearing

lesbian feminists begin to talk with a new sense of urgency about the necessity of declaring our difference within the women's movement instead of rendering ourselves invisible for the sake of a greater acceptability for women's (read, heterosexual) projects and issues. In academia, except perhaps in Women's Studies departments and programs, lesbian faculty continue to render themselves invisible, and teaching or writing critically on overtly lesbian texts tends still to be considered death to an academic career. There is by now a rapidly growing body, a tradition, a culture of lesbian writing that most students are never made aware of.

By featuring women writers from marginalized cultures, the TELLING IT conference was a direct challenge to invisibility. With the hope of eventually being able to edit a proceedings—and thus to carry the dialogue one step further—we recorded the panels, workshops, performances and readings at the conference. At that point it was merely a hope; two years later we have in this book a transformation of the conference

The Editing Collective

Faced with some sixteen hours of recorded conference material to sift through, the question was, how should editing of all this material be done? A collective process seemed like the best approach, and Sky Lee, Lee Maracle and Betsy Warland, three of the writers who lived in Vancouver and who represented each of the three communities featured at the conference, agreed to form an editing collective with me.

When the transcripts started coming in we realized that we had far more material than we could include in a single volume. After much discussion, we decided that we would not attempt to edit a proceedings of the conference—or at least that the proceedings would be only partial. What we were most interested in doing was furthering the discussion of issues that were raised at the conference. We wanted the book to stand as a more developed contribution to the discussion that has been raging in various communities across the country on what kind of relationship might be possible between cultures of colour and white culture, between lesbian culture and heterosexist mainstream culture. To this end we decided that Lee, Betsy and Sky would each write a commentary from her own point of view, taking up issues from the conference workshops and panel discussions but writing beyond the immediate scope of the conference. Their commentaries, as it turns out, contain some of the most passionate, concise and sustained analysis in the book.

As a collective we had to work our way through issues that arose out of different cultural values. In fact, these cultural differences came into play at every level and with every decision. At first it was a shock to realize that what i took as a given, whether we were talking about a grammatical issue such as the use of pronouns, or an editing issue such as whether to cut or include a particular comment from the audience and why, only reflected *my* set of cultural assumptions. There were moments when either Sky or Lee presented such a different way of looking at the subject under discussion that i felt that definite unease you feel when the ground of your sense of the real is shaken. This can feel threatening. It can also feel very exciting, because it augurs a contextual shift so basic it shakes the edifice of values we live inside of. As two white women and two women of colour, it seems to me that we were working hard to break through the stereotypes we represented for each other, caught as we are on opposite sides of the abyss of racism.

This abyss, and the issue of cultural difference which it raises, is exactly the site of discussion for this book. Lee has used the image of unfinished ramparts, earthworks, leading to a never-completed bridge that might span this abyss. *Telling It* is offered as one small extension of the necessary earthworks for that bridge.

PART ONE

Voices From the Conference

PANEL ONE

Across the Cultural Gap

*Panelists:**
Jeannette Armstrong
Betsy Warland
Lee Maracle

What are the difficulties and pleasures of writing in a language and to a culture different from your own?
How does the spiritual become political?
What are the implications of working in the genres of repressed traditions that are not recognized by mainstream culture as legitimate?

---

*Editors' note: A fourth writer who participated on this panel has chosen not to have her talk included in this book.

Words

Jeannette Armstrong

photo: Evelyn Fingarson

I'm really happy to have made it here; I was really looking forward to this time to hear the other speakers and also to take part in this conference. When I was asked whether I would attend and speak on this topic in particular, I was really excited about it because it's one of the areas I think about a lot, not only in terms of my writing but in the work that I do in my life. I think about it in terms of the people I affect in my work, the words I speak and the words I write. What I would like to do is go back and talk a little bit about my history, how it has shaped my thinking and how my writing was impacted by my traditional background.

I was one of the lucky people on my reservation. I was born into a traditional family: my family is an old family in the Okanagan with a long history. They were given responsibilities that date back thousands of years. Because of those responsibilities, they kept certain parts of our culture and our traditions alive and handed them down to other people in the Okanagan, to other children of generations coming. As a result, my family took a really hard line on independence during the colonial process and withstood real hardship during the past one hundred years of brutality that all my people in Canada and the United States shared.

As a youth, I did not understand why my family were the way they were. I remember as a teenager that I began to understand the value of being who I am, an Okanagan woman, a person who has been educated and taught things that other people did not have access to. Many of our people were coerced and brutalized for speaking their language and practicing their culture until their memory grew distant and dim. Over the years my family was able to separate us from that in many ways.

My grandmother refused to speak English all her life. I really admire her for that. She refused to acknowledge any English word from any of us, refused to allow my father and my uncles and my sisters to receive any sort of white education, in any way. At the time my father was a child, the government was taking Native children by force and putting them in residential schools. They were called agricultural schools at that time. The children raised pigs, they raised potatoes and they fed the nuns and priests—really well. My father did not attend these schools. He married and had children when the provincial government was coercing people in our communities, forcibly removing the children and putting them into residential schools at Kamloops, and they resisted that.

There was a huge battle. There are newspaper accounts of this mini-war that happened in our community, right on our reserve. The traditional people who were not adherents of the Catholic Church just refused, said "No, we're not letting our children be taken." My father stood by that, but at the same time he knew and realized that the world was changing, that there was a need for his children to be able to speak our language *and* learn to survive in this world where English is a must. He spoke to the people, the traditional leadership in the community, and said there needed to be schools on the reservation and only then would his children attend.

My oldest sister was twelve years old when she first attended school and she learned English in grade one; she never spoke English until then. She would come home and teach us English. I was bilingual by the time I entered first grade, bilingual in the sense that I understood ten percent of what the teacher was saying—the rest of it was pretty hard to catch. It was difficult to learn the language. It was difficult to attend school within a system in which everything was taught in English. But I had a great love for learning and I was excited about anything, whether it was the English language or whether it was geometry.

I enjoyed my school years, but I realized at that time that there was a big difference, a huge difference between the way my people taught and how the teacher was thinking. There was a large difference between what the village people were thinking and saying and what this teacher was thinking and saying. I think it's that background that has given me the strength to be able to find myself, my voice. My background of tradition and resistance enables me to present myself in the way that I do in my writing.

It took a long time for me to realize the value of having a grandmother who could speak to me in the total purity of our language, the total purity of the words which have been handed down through thousands of years from mind to mind, from mouth to mouth, encompassing actions generated for I don't know how long—thousands and thousands of years. I was given an understanding of how a culture is determined, how culture is passed on. It *is* through words, it *is* through the ability to communicate to another person, to communicate to your children the thinking of your people in the past, their history, that you *are* a people. The words of my people are significant to me, to my understanding and to my dignity as a person, to my ability to differentiate and look at the world and say: "This is what I agree with and this is what I can choose to care about and this is what I can choose to rage against."

I feel fortunate to have been given that. I realize I am much more fortunate than a lot of other Native people who didn't have the benefit of their own language and nevertheless had the benefit of elders and their teachings in a second language. I can go back now and look at the world and see a real difference between our ways and the ways of this world. It's hard for me to articulate this: I'm still trying to find ways to articulate what this difference does to me internally, what the two languages do to me inside. It's difficult for me to talk about it *this* way, because our language is made up of metaphor. When we speak to each other, when we communicate with one another, we are communicating something that's coming from thought, something that's coming from no [physical] thing. You're taking something that's nothing and you're attempting to make it visual, familiar to another person's sense of touch, feeling, taste, sight or whatever. You're attempting to take something that's not physical and turn it into a physical experience for another person. In doing that we draw on ways that will enable us to do it in the best possible way, so that the person can understand what you're saying as familiarly as possible given this particular human being's already existing feelings.

We find ways to do that. We find ways to couch our transmission of information to other people in metaphor. Some of these metaphors in cultures become archetypes, or become symbols that are passed on from generation to generation. When I say a word that may have no meaning for another culture, it has huge meaning for me. When I say "coyote" it has a huge 20,000 year meaning behind it that has been passed on and on and on. Our character, our world view, the relationship we have to each other as a people, our humanness towards the world and how we relate to the spiritual is wrapped up in the metaphors we use. All things hold meaning only in terms I understand, so that when I say "coyote" to you and in your mind you see some four-legged creature running around, usually pretty rag-tag looking, you know that that coyote has a whole different meaning for you than it does for me. Your experience is different.

Speaking across the cultural gap has become a challenge and a way for me to speak to those of my people who share the experiences of our history, our culture, in a way that they can understand. I learn this [English] language so that I can say to Indigenous people, this is what my people understand. This is how I have experienced it in these words I give you. I choose to share these words in the English language with anyone who speaks English, but especially with my people.

I do write for my people. I do at all times speak to my people when I'm writing. Whenever I waver from that I get lost; I can't speak to the newcomers and when I do it becomes dangerous because I don't know your metaphors. I don't know what your thinking is, what your perceptions are, and I don't know how to approach that. It's still very confusing to me, sometimes, when I look at your culture. It sometimes seems pretty strange . . . but I understand the reverse of that is also true. So when I look at the special meanings of words I think about watching my mother and before her my grandmother as they speak, as they present themselves. Their words were very carefully chosen and very carefully constructed. When you speak, when you take language and put it out for someone to come up against, you not only have to assume responsibility for speaking those words, but you are responsible for the effect of those words on the person you are addressing *and* the thousands of years of tribal memory packed into your understanding of those words. So, when you speak, you need to know what you are speaking about. You need to perceive or imagine the impact of your words on the listener and understand the responsibility that goes with *being* a speaker.

Sometimes I am really fearful and find myself in really dangerous territory when speaking words because of the obvious: words can be misconstrued. One of my greatest fears when I wrote *Slash*—not so much the children's books because I was really on familiar territory there, I worked with a lot of elders to write those books—was to have Native people read it. Yet, it was for them that I wrote it. I didn't care what non-Indian people said about it. Lee Maracle's one of the few people whose reading of it I feared. It was not the fear of being put down, but the terror of being misunderstood because I was using the English language and not my own.

Spirituality is very, very clearly tied in with my purpose of being, as an Okanagan woman, born into this world at this time. I am still searching for my own purpose, but I understand I have been given an ability to speak two languages, to cross between these two languages in my mind. I also understand that our language comes from a sacred place. I don't understand where the English language originates, yet, but when Native people think about the source of thought we consider the vast pool of creation and its origin. We think about the things that formed us as thinking, human, walking people, different from the animal people. When we consider the spiritual place from which our thinking arises, the words become sacred things because they come from that place. My responsibility is to strive for correctness in my presentation, correctness of purpose and accuracy in my use of words in my attempt to transcend the simple actuality of the things I have seen, to the image of those same things in the context of my entire history and the sacred body of knowledge that we, as a people, have acquired.

Words have been used to destroy, to cause pain, to cause

the kinds of things that we see happening all over the world between people, between individuals, between races, between sexes, even between fat and skinny people. Many words do that. My responsibility is to approach all these phenomena, all of this colossal misuse of words from my purpose as part of a healing process for my children and my people who have been so damaged, so brutalized that their language, their tongues, have been wrenched from their mouths in the past one hundred years. I strive to be able to return some of those words, whether in English or in Okanagan, to inspire the return of our abilities, to put a framework around thinking that is good and healthy for our people, so that my children, my grandchildren and my great-grandchildren will have the benefit of a healthier world.

We are all responsible in that way. We are all thinking people. We all have that ability and we all have that responsibility. We may not want to have that responsibility or we may feel unworthy of that responsibility, but every time we speak we have that responsibility. Everything we say affects someone, someone is hearing it, someone is understanding it, someone is going to take it and it becomes memory. We are all powerful, each one of us individually. We are able to make things change, to make things happen differently. We are all able to heal.

All of what I have said is central to my writing, my thinking and my approach to life.

f.) is sure

Betsy Warland

photo: Evelyn Fingarson

I'm going to play around with the title of our panel called "Across the Cultural Gap," and look at some related clichés and sayings. ***To blow the gap***, give information. Gap: an opening; a fissure; a break or pass through the mountains; a suspension of continuity; a conspicuous difference; a space traversed by an electrical spark; from Old Norse, chasm; to open the mouth, yawn. I love how etymologies always seem to take us back to the mouth! So, here we are, talking about the mouth again. Yes, I have to wonder what the "yawn" is about and I suspect what it calls up is how we deal with difference among ourselves. After we've first encountered difference and recovered from the initial terror, I think that what we often do is quickly move into a stance of saying, oh it's boring to talk about this again; it's wearing; it's a drag; let's talk about something interesting—which is usually yet another topic about ourselves.

So, across the cultural mouth. It is a cross we bear, this supposed collective mouth we're repeatedly told represents us all. We know who makes it through the "opening," who "pass"(es), which rhymes with blast—we know who has the dynamite power in the mountains of our collective teeth. We know who has the electrically amplified voices. Those of us here are whispers in the collective head. We're the voices that make the jaw clench.

To stop two gaps with one bush. This is an Old English saying which is actually another version of "to kill two birds with one stone." More and more has been written about feminine writing in the fissure—a writing which is attempting to no longer beat around the bush, around some topics, and we're becoming—think of the word "fissure,"—(f.), for the feminine gender, is sure! That's what's beginning to happen I think with some of these voices. It's no coincidence that most of the language-focused and language-concerned women writers who are feminists in English Canada come to the English language at a slant, to use a phrase of Emily Dickinson's. This is often because we're writing from a second language or culture and/or race. For some of us, the disparity is not obvious. For instance, I'm a blond, blue-eyed, middle-class, White, stereotype Western woman. I'm the image that is invariably trotted out to make the points about racism and sexism.

To stop the gap, secure a weak point; prevent attack. When I was thirty years old I finally realized that I speak English as a second language—this is not metaphorically speaking—this is actually true. It's not a coincidence that I realized this during the same period of time that I came out as a lesbian because it was, in fact, my first woman lover who pointed this out to me. It made sense, finally, of why I always have difficulty with grammar and sentence structure. I seldom construct a sentence in the way that I should—at least in the beginning. It also made sense of why it's so difficult for me to speak in public without notes or a written text that I can rework and revise (which I do a lot of) ahead of time. And even when I'm on a one-to-one basis and I'm really involved in an intense conversation around ideas

(I'm OK with emotions), but with ideas—the words just blow away: gone! I spend half my brain time trying to catch them again. The reason is because I grew up in a Norwegian, rural community. My grandparents all came from Norway; that whole generation came from Norway. My parents were the first generation to grow up speaking both languages and my generation was the first to speak English as our mother tongue. But I was learning English from people who were all speaking it as a second language. They were trying valiantly to imitate what they thought was proper English. This was in the U.S. and there was a tremendous pressure. You felt compelled to be a part of the melting pot; to fit in, to "pass." On top of this, all the important adult conversations occurred in Norwegian but we were not allowed to learn Norwegian, so there was a real double message there. So, it's like I have this invisible pattern of the Norwegian language implanted on my brain yet I don't even know the language.

Next, in terms of language, came my experience as an incest victim. I learned very profoundly that language is not to be trusted. It is all too often a vehicle for deception. If I stated my reality, it was totally denied, so my choice was to withdraw into myself. My silence was all I had to protect me from losing myself and my reality. It was the only way I could keep clear about what was really going on. It took me 34 years to even begin to remember this: that's how severe the repression of this painful experience was. My first memory came back to me with a single word echoing in my head, the word "hotel." No, it wasn't "just a game."

To open the gap, give access to. More recently, my experience as a lesbian and its impact on my sense and use of the English language has affected me as a writer. In my first book, *A Gathering Instinct* (which came out in 1981), the last three poems in that book were the first poems I wrote as a lesbian. They were love poems and they were intentionally non-gendered, universal love poems—so you couldn't really tell anything about the gender of either lover. This was intentional because I was afraid. Later, as I became more grounded in my life as a lesbian, and my vision as a lesbian, I came smack up against the reality that there were no words for my experience—my erotic, sexual and spiritual experiences as a lesbian. In my second book, *open is broken* (which came out in 1984), I started to sink myself into language; I began to take it apart and make up words and reclaim it. That's when I came into a deep realization that language is a value system. It's not neutral. It's a value system created and maintained by patriarchal, White, middle-class, heterosexual, educated people who generally tyrannize the rest of the world. My understanding of this language/power structure has profoundly shaped my work ever since.

To stand in the gap, act as defender. Those of us working with language, and consequently form (often the two go together), are increasingly being criticized. I was actually surprised when Viola [Thomas] commented on that. But it's true. And, in fact, there's been hostility lately. This often comes from other women writers, many of them feminists, who say things like "leave the language alone; it's perfectly adequate—you're just covering up bad writing." [laughter from audience and panel]. Sounds familiar? Many of them say that the tradition and the mainstream present no problems for them as women writers. I'm not necssarily in argument with their experiences, but I am in argument with their criticisms, because we are told that our writing is negative, narrow, patriarchy-bashing, and that it's for "card carrying members." In fact, those of us involved in experimenting with language in English Canada—well, our relationships are very erratic; some of us rarely even talk to each other. Most of us don't really know each other very well—so this last criticism is pretty bizarre. A criticism which came up recently in an interview with several B.C. women writers was that there's only one person to do this, "and everybody else is just like a cookie cutter."[1] This "one person" is Nicole Brossard, whose work I greatly admire. But to me this judgement smells of tokenism—like there can only be one lesbian writer who can do language-focused writing. In fact, a lot of the language-focused writers in English Canada aren't lesbian or White, but this doesn't matter, right? We all sort of look alike: you can't really tell the difference—there's only one that's authentic. Which probably translates into the mainstream only wanting to deal with one: one's enough! What all this is about is fear. Fear blurs our vision. When we are afraid, we cannot perceive the specifics of difference. We can only perceive our fear.

The criticism I feel the most angry about is when I hear that feminist language-focused writers are being "prescriptive," even, it's been said (in the same interview), "morally prescriptive." This is The Great Reversal! This is a strategy from the patriarchy—where you turn things around and accuse others of the very thing you're doing. The tradition in the mainstream is to assert (and believe) that art is not prescriptive or political. The norm is not political, right? It's just the norm. But, they say to writers who are working outside the mainstream, our writing is political: our writing isn't really literature. This goes for Women writers of Colour, lesbian-feminist writers, language-focused writers, whatever. And I'm saying that we must not be intimidated and silenced by these criticisms, even when they come from women who are friends and acquaintances, even when we feel betrayed, even when it hurts like hell.

A cultured mouth. Culture, Latin, cultura, cultivate, to loosen the earth around plants to destroy the weeds. Point of view: who are the plants and who are the weeds? Point of vision: why don't we all be weeds? Now that's when writing gets interesting, you know. We need all the dialects, ***to fill in the gap***, make up a deficiency, fill in a vacant space. Because we are absent in the English language as women who are self-defined and named. So, we're free to invent, reclaim, redis-cover language on a word-to-word basis: like children—the power, the sensuousness and the magic of words. This is where language becomes very spiritual for me; when it is not a given but a gift.

Sources

1. Constance Rooke, "Getting into Heaven: An Interview with Diana Hartog, Paulette Jiles, and Sharon Thesen," *The Malahat Review* 83 (Summer 1988).

Just Get in Front of a Typewriter and Bleed

Lee Maracle

photo: Evelyn Fingarson

Betsy wanted to play with the topic, but I think I will dissect it and separate it out—just a little bit. "What are the difficulties and pleasures of writing in a language different from your own?" I think I understand what the organizers are trying to ask, at least I optimistically hope that I understand what they are trying to ask. I want to clarify something: it is not any more difficult for Native people to learn English than it is for an English person to learn French or even English, at least in terms of writing. I have a favorite saying. I stuck it just above my typewriter, where I can see it: "Writing is easy, you just get in front of a typewriter and bleed."[1]

Historically, the difficulty for us in mastering this language was that it was not accessible to us. Until the last four decades we were not taught to write English. Now I know everyone is going to gasp and say that Native people who went to residential school were forced to speak English. That's only half the truth. Native people were prohibited from speaking their own language in residential schools that were little better than religious farms in which the students were servants. My sister spent years praying at convent school, cooking delicious pies and ironing the starched paraphernalia of the nunnery and the priesthood, along with dozens of other Native girls. She left school at fifteen, functionally illiterate, but a great cook and laundress, which by the way is how she made her living throughout her short life. Like prisoners, the students learned about shoe-making, horse-shoeing, orchardry and so forth, but received very little academic instruction. It was in the context of not being taught English that the prohibition of our language was a most bitter pill to swallow.

By the early fifties, our parents and grandparents were divided about the value of education. Some, returning virtually languageless, resented being forced to speak a language they were never adequately taught; others, as a result both of the prohibition of their own language and the cutting off of their tribal education at six years old, having no words in which to imagine why Indians had to suffer hardship after hardship, committed suicide. Everything white became bad for them. Still others refused to teach their children their own language, lest they should bring undue suffering to their children, lest their children become "crippled two-tongues," children without language.

The difficulty for myself has been mastering a language different from my own, without having my own. Most of us learned English from parents who spoke English in translation. Many of our parents had been to residential school and thus did not speak the old language any better than the average five-year-old speaks English. Without academic instruction and without their own language there were no words to articulate complex thoughts, passions or ideas. All of that is like playing football with a handicap: difficult, but not impossible.

Even greater difficulty is due to the nature of the English language itself. I hereby recognize that there are elder Canadian women in the audience—I hope you are not offended by some of the next language here. It is a pretty ugly language. "Fuck" is an oft-used graphic, expressing a multitude of emotions for the Canadian population. It expresses fear, surprise, anger, delight, even wonderment. Witness: "Fuck YOU," "OH fuck," "Fucking-A, man" and so forth. This word is one of the most colourful possessors of multiple meanings in this language. I bring it up because I once looked up the source of the word and it is very important that women remember this. (I was curious about the obsession of the general population to reduce their language to a simplistic catchall that has sexual connotations.) The origins of the word are frightening. It originates in law. This acronym means: For Un-Carnal Knowledge, literally child rape—and our children use it very, very often. The perverse sense of sexuality of this society is structured into the everyday language that we use.

It is really difficult to learn this language for all the good citizens of this country. It is true that Native people leave school earlier than do white people, but we often have a better grasp of the essence of the language than do a good many Canadians who graduate from high school. As environmentalists, as natural people, we have difficulty churning out reams of useless propaganda that amount to so much form-filling in elementary school, but we are not defeated by the obstacles put in our path to acquire English words. As orators, we are not as short on vocabulary as a good may Canadians are. I am a classic example. I was raised to be exactly what I am: a Native intellectual. I did not complete high school, but because I was taught to respect language in general and despite the fact that this language was not my own, I learned it well.

Our best orators, in English or their own language, are those who have struggled with the language unencumbered by the tedious commas and colons of the English language. I always wonder what the relationship is between colon in the human body and that little pause in the language. I don't really understand what the relationship is, but I wonder about it. I urge you to attend the assemblies of First Nations. Listen to the likes of Simon Lucas, Simon Baker... I am also reminded of Jeannette's parents... Their command of this language, the meaning they infuse it with, is extraordinary. Read *My Heart Soars* by Dan George, not merely an actor, but a poet orator supreme, so supreme that Canada invited him to write and deliver the soliloquy for Canada's 100th (sic) birthday. It is a beautiful rendering of the historic aspirations of our people that were interrupted by colonization and the failure of Canada to walk in our shoes and learn from us. My ancestors, despite all obstacles, have done for your language what Shakespeare intended—rendered it just, laced it with social and natural conscience and transformed it into a language of the future. We did not say "mankind"—the word is "people." We avoid the graphic "fuck," and we restore to the language its sense of social discipline that all languages begin with.

"What are the difficulties and pleasures of writing in a culture not you own?" Well, to tell the truth, I don't write in or to a culture not my own. I write to and from my own. If I forget that for a minute, if I stray from that for a second, my writing would be useless to all, including you. 'Tis Canadians, most of all white Canadians, that need to walk a mile in my moccasins. Most white Canadians lack the intimate knowledge of the self that could transform this world of unbridled waste and butchery of spirit into a world rich with social and natural conscience. Those of us who have not left ourselves behind can be a valuable service to you, but only if we write from our own culture.

"How does the spiritual become political?" This is a deadly question. I think it's one that can only be answered from the position of standing in the center of a circle and embracing every direction at the same time. If I could answer you, I would be the greatest healer in history. It belongs most properly to the realm of mass and natural healing, a huge cleansing ceremony that our mother earth and all her children acting directly on her natural behalf alone can answer. It is an historic question that I feel unable to answer, but I will say this: politics arises out of law. Politically oppressed people struggle in the context of law to change the laws of the oppressor so as to free themselves and become unhindered. Spirit is what moves all living things. Everyone is motivated spiritually to move in a given political direction. The process, the how of it, I am not up to speculating about.

"What are the implications of working in genres of repressed traditions that are not recognized by mainstream cultures as legitimate?" That is simple. You don't sell many books. I think I do things for this language that say, Louis L'Amour (if that be his real name), cannot do, but I doubt I will ever be as well read in my lifetime. I will not change my writing for all that, however. I choose to write the sorts of things that are durable, hopefully enlightening, and hopefully useful historically. I doubt that Louis L' Amour will be regarded as a great writer representing his generations's best literature some hundred years down the road. I want to be the kind of writer that will be read by generations of children to come. Whether or not I succeed is immaterial—I am very conscious that here lie dead trees. More: I want this world to never forget its short but cruel history of racial, national and sexual oppression.

Sources

1. James Charlton, ed., *Writers' Quotation Book* (New York: Penguin Books, 1980).

Panel One: Audience Discussion

Viola Thomas, Moderator
photo: Evelyn Fingarson

C.L. DI MARCO: I'm a freelancer myself in different areas—writing has been one of them—and what I find as far as discrimination is concerned, when I write my full name I seldom get responses. When I write a pseudonym or initials, I get responses. And I'm talking about for the same writing, the same words for the same editors. I fool around like that a lot until they catch on that it's the same person. (*laughter*) I feel like as women, we're already being discriminated against, whatever our sexual orientations are—that's another problem—whatever the line of work we do, the amount of education, our cultural backgrounds. I'm just wondering if that happens to any of you up there?

LEE MARACLE: I notice I always get a response, but that's because most editors think I'm a Mr. Lee Maracle. I always get a Mr. Lee Maracle back, even though I put Ms. I agree that if you're not male and you're not English, you do rarely get a response.

DOROTHY LIVESAY: Well I am obviously WASP, but I have had

trouble with names, so I have two names—my birth name, Dorothy Livesay, which I started writing and publishing under, and then my married name, Macnair, and I've found it a great help. Because I've been known as an agitator, the name Dorothy Livesay means my letters just don't get printed. (*laughter*) But if I write as a helpless old lady (*laughter*) they'll gladly say Mrs. Macnair or, I hope not Ms., I hate the prefix Ms., I think it's just disgraceful. (*laughter*)

PEG KLESNER: I'd like to just say a word or two about what a previous speaker* said about lesbians, because I have a little different viewpoint in terms of the conference. I felt that we were coming as exploring writers in cultures rather than writers in languages. I mean obviously we're talking about languages but as a lesbian—and this is the first time I've ever said it publicly (*applause*)—I feel very strongly that we have a very long oral tradition of lesbian culture which we need to share with other women because we are indeed a network of loving people and we need to understand each other. When we identify ourselves as lesbian writers or as Native writers or as Punjabi writers, we have differences that we can share to enlarge our own understanding of women in general.

. . .

LOUISE PROFEIT-LEBLANC [speaking from the audience]: I just want to say that I'm really happy to be here and I'm so happy with all the presentations that have been made this afternoon, I've learned a lot. And with regards to the pamphlet:** I work for a male director and when I first approached him about

---

*This speaker has asked to be deleted from the transcript of the audience discussion. In her comments, she questioned the inclusion of lesbian writers in the conference. She wondered how lesbians could constitute a culture since lesbians lack their own language. Her missing comments will be indicated by ellipses.

**The brochure advertising the conference.

coming to this conference, as soon as he saw the word lesbian he said you're not going to that conference and we're not giving you time off to go. So I was very happy to hear it said that we are all women here and we are all voices that should be heard. And anyway, I managed to talk to his deputy minister and talk some sense into him. (*laughter*) But the other thing about this naming business: I've been very involved in my own community with oral tradition. My family name is Profeit and I come also from a very large traditional family of Profeits and when I first began to work on radio my name was Louise Profeit. Shortly after I got married I decided I'll just switch over to Louise LeBlanc. It was really funny because when I announced over the radio, this is Louise LeBlanc signing off until next week or whatever, my phone started ringing at home and the elders who had given me full trust, they said, who's that lady on the radio? (*laughter*) So I hyphenated my name and it's really interesting that the more you use it, the more people begin to understand your so-called professional name.

. . .

BETSY WARLAND: I know the difference between what it was like to be a white, straight, heterosexual woman writer and what it's like now to be a lesbian writer. It's a big difference and there is a lot of discrimination. In fact I am working to develop a dialect in my language so it reflects me, just as Jeannette spoke, all of us have spoken about how difficult that is. But I must be named. I am not nameless and I wouldn't come to this conference if I didn't have my name. I know that it's perhaps hard for other people, but for me I must have my name because it is who I am.

LEE MARACLE: I think that there's a thing that we do in our lives, I think I'm really a victim of it sometimes myself—it's called being erased. And I get up and keep rewriting myself on the blackboard. It used to happen to me when I was a little kid.

I'd put up my hand and because, you know, I was this Indian kid, well obviously I wouldn't know the right answer, so my teachers used to erase me quite consistently. Eventually I was really down, I didn't want anybody to look at me. But after, you know, when I started to have children, well they rewrite you, they really do. You have to look at them every day and you see yourself twenty years ago. I don't think anybody needs to be erased. If a person wants to be identified as a lesbian or doesn't want to be I think that's solely up to them. And if people can't handle that then we've got the kind of society that needs to erase someone. (*applause*)

LESLIE KOMORI: Lee, you were talking about how you feel like your family is between two languages and how that's really crippling but that *is* your culture and that *is* your family and your language. How do you reclaim the power of your culture when you don't really have the language but there is still language there? Because, to be heard, to be understood, you have to speak plain WASP English, you can't have this sort of mushy language that's a mix of the language of your ancestors and the English language. How do you relate the power of your culture when you don't have that pure language?

LEE MARACLE: I think we're getting into what you consider magic now; I don't. Our people believe that memory is passed on in more ways than words. We firmly believe that our grandmothers' voices are still alive and in this room, that they are everywhere and the individual *can* reach back and hear those voices. I don't think that there is any way except through ceremony to do that, whether you have your language or not. I have seen children who should not know their language come forward with songs in ceremony and I have had this experience myself. We have our own way of hearing those voices. It's always a trouble, I think, to really realize a full self.

JILLIAN RIDINGTON: I've been around the women's movement

for a long time. I happen to be heterosexual but I think that one of the biggest gaps in the women's movement all these years has been between women who are heterosexual and lesbians. This is about closing the gaps. There *are* differences in languages, there *are* differences in experience, and we need to talk about them, we need to understand each other so that those gaps that people try and make between women become bridged. I think it's very important to have lesbian women talking about their experience, where it differs, where their language differs, so that we *can* come to those understandings. This bridge is just as important as the bridge between any two cultures.

BARBARA BINNS: I'm not a writer, I'm not a lesbian, but I'm a woman of colour and this has to do with the first statement in the brochure. It started off by saying women of colour and lesbian women. Well my first reaction was, oh my god, here we go again. It presupposes that women who are of colour are not lesbian (*applause*), and this happens over and over again. I do wish when you use the language, you become very sensitive to the issue you're trying to address.

. . .

ANONYMOUS: Somebody mentioned the word WASP and one of the things I have a great amount of difficulty with is that because the colour of my skin is light it is assumed immediately that I am a White, Anglo-Saxon, Protestant. Well, only the first initial is correct for me and I find that that label erases my identity totally. I have put a great amount of hard work into mastering the English vocabulary and trying to speak with the minimum amount of accent that I can achieve because that's the way to survive, and I would like credit for that and not just be told, oh well, you're WASP, you don't count. And secondly, I would like to say to Lee that not knowing one's own soul is the equivalent of not having one and that is what has been said about women all the time. In 1920 or whenever we went for the vote, we were told you do not have a soul and that's also about being erased.

LEE MARACLE: I don't think because you don't understand your soul that's equivalent to not having one. I still—and I think Jeannette made this point as well—am searching for that self, that soul. I'd also like to say that I use the term white, not WASP. I use that term just the same way you say indigenous, and there are many cultures of indigenous people in this country, even in this province. I don't mean it in a derogatory sense.

C.L. DI MARCO: It seems like the whites are just as worried about being discriminated against as anybody else. I am trilingual and I feel like we're all here together. It bugs me to hear that we're all worried about being discriminated against, even though that's true. I feel that rather than referring to each other as being white, black, brown, whatever colour we are and thinking of it as derogatory, I like to think of it as being positive because we add to culture.

KAY BREMNER [addressing the panel]: In your personal exploration of your differences, have you found any similarities?

JEANNETTE ARMSTRONG: I have been just sitting listening to the comments that have been made, because some of it doesn't make a lot of sense to me because of the question that you're asking. I guess in the last ten years I have started to ask some questions not only of myself and of my people as a cultural group, but of my people as people from this land and from this earth and as living parts of this universe. And I think that when we start looking at what we are, rather than which race, what sex, what colour, what size, I think we start to come to those universals, we start to begin to speak the real language and that real language is a language that is understood by babies and is known between people as relationships. That language has more to it than words. I think when we begin to get to that point, then we can begin to cross these cultural and racial and social and class and size gaps. I'm serious about that. We haven't a clue about what we are, we're just beginning to open our eyes and maybe understand that we are human and a part of something much vaster and more beautiful than we can hope to know in a lifetime. All kinds of people and their thinking are a part of that so I have a hard time with this racial thing. I know I rage against it, I speak out against it, because it's those things that stop our world from being what it could be and should be and probably will be if we keep talking like this.

. . .

LEE MARACLE: I think the last three words of my talk we have in common—a struggle against national, sexist, and racist oppression. That's what we have in common, whether it takes one form or another. I also would like to mention that the women here, Betsy, Viola, myself and Jeannette are all examples of how greatly we have struggled to master a language that has no respect for us and I can tell you that in this room there are very few white people who can put up their hands and say they speak Punjabi, Cree, Okanagan, etc. Do you understand what I'm saying? That we're not speaking from a position of equals here. What's at the very bottom line of overcoming any kind of discrimination is a real coming together where a real exchange takes place. Not just my having to come to *you* but when do you cross *my* bridge? I welcome you to it. (*applause*)

UNIDENTIFIED SPEAKER: I have a couple of comments to make about how the panel's been speaking and I'd like people to think about it because we're all learning from each other. One thing is the use of the word "master" which really turns me off. It's one of the words on that list I'm trying to figure out how to work out of my language because it has so many implications—like the word "peasant" and a few others that have a lot of class or religious connotation in the Canadian language. The second thing is your comment about learning to speak so that it's healing: I think that's a beautiful way to think. Because of the way religious teaching or other cultural teaching has been, there's a tendency to say, don't say anything until you have it all together. I really appreciate the Native people that I've met, that they speak so slowly, use few words—I'm learning from that. People do try to put pressure on us to do things fast, faster all the time, speak fast and understand fast, and it's kind of like the lemmings jumping off the cliff, you know. If they can make you go fast enough you won't really know what you're doing and you can be taken advantage of. That's not always intentional but it definitely seems to be the way it goes.

ANTOINETTE WINKELMAN: Lee Maracle has just asked when are we going to cross that bridge to the place where language has been used to wrench the words out of people's mouths. The sacred place where language comes from has been pointed out by Jeannette Armstrong. If we are to attempt to cross the bridge, we who are not Native people, we have to be very careful not to be appropriating language that does not naturally belong to us. Yet there is this very delicate possibility of being able to be healed by the knowledge that has been established over so many hundreds of years. What kind of advice could you give to the non-Native writers about how we could very carefully learn from your language without appropriating or harming it any more?

JEANNETTE ARMSTRONG: There was a similar question asked in Montreal [at the Third International Feminist Bookfair, June 1988]. First of all, we do as Native writers suffer because of the kind of cultural imperialism that's taking place when non-Native people speak about Native ceremony and Native thinking, Native thought, Native life style, Native world view and speak as though they know what they are speaking about. That's appropriation of culture because no one can experience and know what I know and experience or what my grandmother knows or what Lee knows and feels, and she can speak with her own voice and so can I and so could my grandmother. But I understand that when we attempt to speak to one another and understand one another there *is* a point at which bridges must be crossed both ways and that is where, for me, it's very difficult. I know that you can speak to another person without appropriating and I know a lot of it has to do with listening first of all, listening and understanding and waiting till that understanding has reached a point at which you can say, do you mean this and that person says yes, I mean this. It's as simple as that, I think.

ELIZABETH FORTES: I want to thank all of you for the tremendous presence and honesty of your presentations, because it suddenly became possible to go beyond the cultural gap. I'm one of those who have learned to speak English after arriving in this country. It's been a tremendous struggle to learn to speak it and to hear my own accent echoing through these walls and then to get closer to working with Native people and feeling apologetic for my accent because I'm suddenly an outsider. The way one speaks the language is the way one's trying to live this language in this country. And it's a tremendous amalgamation that one is trying to make to rebuild oneself. We don't know who we are up to this point, but we know who we are in the process of becoming. There are thousands of women out there who still cannot write—cannot write in their own language and cannot write in English—so they cannot read. I just wanted to remind all of us that they've got to be here too.

BETSY WARLAND: One last remark. I want to tell a simple story that happened to me, I don't know how long ago now, seems like another lifetime, when Martin Luther King was assassinated. I'm originally from the U. S. and one of my closest friends then was a Black woman from Chicago named Margaret. I was an art student then and she was the only person of colour in that art department. When Martin Luther King was assassinated I remember we were in class and working on wood cuts and we just all stopped, we could not say anything, do anything, we just sat there. The school screamed to a stop for about a day or two. Our instructor, who was really a very nice guy and had had Margaret often take care of their children—yes, right, you get the drift here—he said to her at one point, Margaret, you're just like me you know, I consider you just like me. He thought this was a compliment, you see, and he was saying it from a sincere, loving heart, but Margaret finally looked at him and said, I'm *not* just like you. That's when that whole conversation in our group turned around in the direction it had to go. What we had been saying as white people was, you're just like me, and when we say that we're saying *you're just like me in all the ways that you're white and I don't really want to know much about the rest of your life*. He knew very little about Margaret's life, her family, where she came from, the community she grew up in, you see. So I think we can't come to this love for each other until we understand our differences, that's the step we can't skip. (*applause*)

LEE MARACLE: I would like to thank everyone for coming here. I would also like to do something that if you were all Native people and I was the younger person sitting up here we would do. I would like to recognize your elders here. I've been to an awful lot of meetings of writers where most of the people are young, lots of times younger than me. But I really think it's a new day in this country when elders, young people and the middle-aged can all be sitting in the same room.

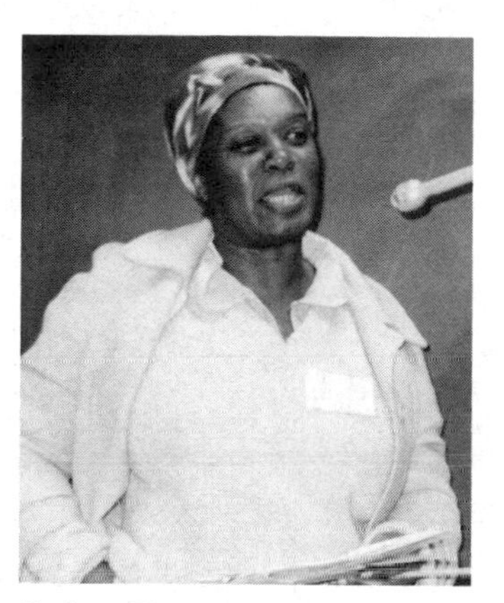

Barbara Binns
photo: Evelyn Fingarson

Leslie Komori
photo: Evelyn Fingarson

(*left to right*) Viola Thomas, Betsy Warland, Lee Maracle, Jeannette Armstrong.
photo: Evelyn Fingarson

Panel One: Creative Writing

Jeannette Armstrong

Wind Women

Maggie at night sometimes I hear you laugh

when I was ten we rode to huckleberry mountain
carrying ragged quilts and pots and pans
packed on an old roan mare called jeep
given to Maggie to help fill her baskets
I followed her
picking berries her failing eyes had missed
I listened as she talked in our language
half singing sometimes
for all the pickers to hear
her voice high and clear in the crisp mountain air
telling about coyote

I know how the trees talk
I said to Maggie
I heard their moaning in the night
while we lie so tiny in our tents
with those tall black pines swaying over us

she told me a story then
of how the woman of the wind
banished by coyote
carried her eternally howling child
tied to her back
as they moved forever through the tree tops
mother crooning to the child

how sometimes she would swoop down in anger
scattering berries off bushes

Maggie told me I had heard
the wind woman sing
she told me that I would remember that song always
because the trees were my teacher

I remember the song clearly
but it is always Maggie's voice singing
her songs
filling my world
with the moan of old dark pines
as the wind woman
that sings to me
follows
with her hungry child
wherever I go

Blood Of My People

blood of my people   courses through   veins
coming to me   through dust   rising and falling
across ages   the dust   that is my people
that is the land   rises   a continuous red line
across people   across time   is what we are
the living   pulsing   walking   earth
inside me   this collection   moves   a brief shadow
under the sun   lifted by air   pushed   by the force
of earth   circling   majestically   silent
this small storm   for one intense   moment
this fragile breath   lifted   to whirl   to dance
to fly   the elusive magic   of weightlessness
catalytic movement   needed   to press   blood
forward   a red liquid   stream   that draws
ground upward   that shakes   earth and dust   to move
to move   a long line   before settling
quietly   back   into   soil

Grief Is Not The Activity That Heals

grief is only   a place   to begin   it is eyes
turned inward   calling up
disfigured babies   injured   battered   defenceless
open   suck   mouths
hunger shrunken stomachs
crooked bodied adolescents   cower   broken
toothed   blue   black   boot marked
tongues hanging   beaten men
bellies spilling guts   gouges
left for eyes   dry   shrivelled   scrotum sacs
mangle breasted women   legs torn asunder
teeth marks for clothes
rotting cancerous figures   float
to the surface   pieces of death
a dredging   upward   of the guttural   primal
keening   containable in no words   no descriptions
a boiling   and distilling   into bitter water
compacted into crystalline droplets of salt
to be expelled
into excruciating   sundrenched   light
the terrible   the hidden   the unbearable

to grieve   is only to find the place   to begin
the forming into words   the unspeakable
the magic   out of which   comes healing
to bring into understanding   into subjugation
the old lies   that scream and scream
to quiet the internal   quivering and shaking
of flesh and bone   the power to dispel the myths
that cling and cling   to stop the continuous
chant and rattle   of the dying   to turn outward
the eyes   into day   landscape of the living
a leaving of horror   a letting go   never to be recalled

to finally reach outward   to restructure   to allow
time   truth   trust   to pull in   warmth
to fill spaces   with quiet   a light brush of lips
across the cheek   of heart against heart
a murmur   a gentle welling up   an unfettering
of laughter   to wear brightness   fresh words
new stories   a song   the silent singing of which
pushes outward   to fill   others   in the place
to come to

This Is For You On Seeing Bluejay Again

I saw him
again I was there calling on word tunes
to get me through
the air was so heavy with it

Sometimes I get lost
in thoughts of better things to come
the heart is a strange animal
it leaps or nestles
at a touch
and I wonder at times what I see
where the magic lies

I have always wanted to be unfettered

Are you free he asked
the question vibrated inward
touching those parts
that never knew how to stand at the edge

Dance with me
he said
while stars bristle upward from a moon dusk lake

Perhaps it's the word tunes that my heart beats to

I never knew how to dance jazz
but I have watched people
float across to the edge
with such ease

Jazz I like its freedom
he said and reached for my hand

it's not about me
it's about music

A timid creature leapt back

I thought of you then
how you must have been
the one you tell me about
the free one
you are not free now
you have become tangled in that web
that stretches to a horizon
as far as I can see
and I am not afraid of you
you can touch me

Out there where they glide on magic feet
to the edge
a hand reaches out
whirls past
and I see a figure
looking at me
I am afraid
I could lose my footing easily out there

Is that why you don't dance he asked

I'm doing all I can
I'm dancing my voodoo all around you
I'm here
he said
watch out for the poison though
one drop can kill
it's everywhere out here

It's that I am not courageous

I'm in a vortex
I want to hold onto something
I hold on to you
I never wanted to turn to dust though
and mortality lurks
in every gesture of permanence

Is that where the poison hides

Bluejay dancers
I have been told
know how to keep moving

I listened to him read
about the woman who could see tomorrow
I knew the little person was bluejay
who talked to her

I wanted it
to go inside
and look out
through bluejay eyes

Is this what the dance is

I am not courageous
I am afraid of losing myself
I am afraid of dust as well you see
there is no poison here
just dust
a dust storm
a dust devil
a tornado
it was in that room
even when he said
think about a tornado what it could do

In that dust storm
just visible I see bluejay
he is dancing
holding out his hand
Come watch this death we defy

I wrote that poem thirteen years ago
lift me   I said then
bluejay dancer and we will laugh

That woman could see
she danced with bluejay once

From The Landscape Of Grandmother

Words are memory
a window in the present
a coming to terms with meaning
history made into now
a surge in reclaiming
the enormity of the past
a piece in the collective experience of time
a sleep in which I try to awaken
the whispered echoes of voices
resting in each word
moving back into dark blue
voices of continuance
countless sound shapings which roll thunderous
over millions of tongues
to reach me
alive with meaning
a fertile ground
from which generations spring
out of the landscape of grandmother
the sharing
in what we select
to remember
the physical power in thought
carried inside silently
pushing forward in each breathing
meaning wished onto tongues
transforming with each utterance
the stuff of our lives
to travel on wind
on air
to bump wetly
against countless tiny drums
to become sound

spasms coursing upward into imagine
there to turn grey silence
into explosions of colour
calling up the real
the physical
the excruciating sweetness of mouth on mouth
the feltness of the things of us
then settling soundless
colourless
into memory
to be hidden there
reaching ever forward into distances unknown
always linking to others
up to the last drum
vibrating into vast silence

Betsy Warland

mOther muse:/«mousa, mosaic»

how do i (w)right you
you i have protected myself from
for so long
even in my crib
listened intently
how you moved from room to room
not wanting to agitate turn turn tension tighter
you were my mOther
so foreign māter-: «matter»
though the world said the opposite
in every book & greeting card
that we were intimates
in( )mates
crying in the basement
dark walls of depression
closing in after i was born
snowless black fields surrounding
your story of how thrilled you were that i was a girl
always about my father's beaming face brown tie
(which you still recall)
as he leaned over and kissed you
where were you you do not speak of yourself
only the cold metal-table covered with other women's blood
six births before me so fast no time to clean up
and me a breech each
year you recount beaming face tie kiss
words as erasure
it was you who taught me to distrust
their surface
you on the telephone like in front of a mirror
applying them again and again to your offspring's images

makeup madeup altered conversations and events only
hours old
i barely recognized myself
cosmetology of your words for the Others' gaze/appraise
and everyone was the Other (including yourself)
we were strangers from the beginning
tormented by our difference
which did not exist

M: «Around 1000 B.C. the Phoenicians and other Semites and Palestines began to use a graphic sign representing the consonant *m*... they named the sign mēm, meaning "*water*"... »

O: «... they gave it the name ᶜayin, meaning "*eye*"... »

D: «... dāleth, meaning "*door*"... »

E: «... hē and used the consonant *h*... »

waiting at the door
entering

R: «... resh, meaning "*head*"... »

crowning
emerging
her door opens wide
MODER?

no,

MOTHER.

«As in the case of Father, the substitution of the *th* for the earlier *d* dates from the beginning of the sixteenth c.»

and what was lost with the *d*?

D: «Corresponding letters—Sanskrit dwr, Celtic duir, Hebrew dāleth,—meant the Door of birth, death, or sexual paradise... in India it was Yoni Yantre, or yantra of the vulva.»

«d»

sensation of

coming up through the earth

self-possession

«th»

sensation of fragility

energy going out from the mouth   hanging in air

waiting for someone to take it

my mOther calls me

through the dusk «youuu-whooo—Betsy—youuu-whooo . . . »

her "you-who" surfs airwaves

my name a slur in comparison

this ōō-ōō irritates & intrigues

one word two syllables   you/affirmation & who/doubt

intimacy & strangeness

rising settling
                    in a single held moment

her daughter   out there   somewhere

in the barn the woods on her horse in the fields

my voice returns

through divide of night & day
                                        «cooomiiing»

shared eroticism of absence

repression the uncut cord between us

i never touched myself never even thought of it

just like the movies

your twin beds

both feet on the floor at all times

did she ever come? (we ask)

the question hooks off

period of certainty

she had *kids* didn't she

question mark
half a bleeding heart

?

Renaissance «re-, again +
nascī, to be born»

change from agriculture-based economy

to commercial and capitalist society

manufacturing arms and movable field artillery

printing the first book—the Gutenberg Bible

burning Joan of Arc

uprising of peasants

expelling Jews from country after country

Luther and Calvin

first circumnavigation of the globe

and Man's discovery of spermatozoon in the microscope

the Fathers' desire—all that virgin land

and with His new found virility

the «d» was replaced

He had the world to invent «in-, on +
venīre, to come»

Mother stayed home

in a house without door

mmmOther
thirty years later

in another country
i hear "youuu-whooos"

in harbour fog horn

& airplane service-call tones

same reversed musical third
of your call-
                    ing

daughter of "you-who"

left

to come

calling no

daughter in the dark

difference = invisibility: the ground of our meeting

in the authorized world as we know it which is the wor(l)d as The Fathers have told it, Woman is invisible—Woman has only been recognizable (that is *noticed*) in her **caricatured, carricare, a kind of vehicle** difference; bull shit, (as they say). . . a shit load

as women, it is *in our difference* that we perceive ourselves and each other: this is the ground of our meeting—what we are not what we don't want to be what we are (unauthorized) what we wish we could be what we are afraid of being

it is *in our invisibility* that we perceive ourselves and each other: difference = invisibility

it is here, at the locus of our greatest injury & distrust, that we make our trembling attempts to *speak our names hear* one another here on this ground of tears

is it any wonder that we feel such a frightening vulnerability; is it any wonder that we turn away?

difference, dis-, apart + ferre, to carry. see bher-, to carry; also to bear children/bher-: bairn, birth, fertile, suffer, burden, bort "beast of burden"

difference is a gendered word/difference is a gender

so, as "liberated women," we "celebrate our differences"—at conferences, events, concerts, in publications, or is it salivate our differences (each celebrant leaving with her monosyllabic celibacy intact)?

everyone knows the adage "never trust a woman" or "women never trust each other"; everyone knows that's what's going on behind our nervous smiles

i fear for us, if we cannot come to grips with how deeply threatened we feel when we encounter differences among ourselves—i fear that our names will only be exchanged with those women most like ourselves

i fear we will continue to look to the face of The Fathers for our comfort (which is our forgetting), for in His Gaze we can slip sweetly into the Amnesia of Woman: we will not see *our pain (which are our possibilities)* mirrored back

divide and con-her

as we encounter difference within the feminist communities we are enraged when our disparate names are denied: we are terrified that we will be rendered invisible yet again in the very place we had held out our hope of finally *being seen*

this is a well-grounded fear, for as women *our difference has meant our invisibility*: experience has given us little reason to trust it

and yet, if we cannot find other ways to respond to each other than with The Fathers' fear and dismissiveness—we will perpetuate our ghostly roles, police ourselves, never know the **bher-, euphoria** of our own substantiveness

will we persist in embracing our *invisibility as a decoy*, never knowing one another beyond the Fathers' caricatures of Woman, or, can we take our *invisibility as a homeopathic remedy* for our fear, step out from behind our bondwoman smiles: own our creative "burden" as we move our hands across the blank page, the empty canvas of Woman?

Lee Maracle

Sister

I die a little to think
we could never be,
            two sisters,
in love with life.
to share the same dream,
the clean, sweet vision
of a people august and free.

I die a little to think
we let them divide us,
we had not the love
            to bind us.
So powerless were we
as small babies, to see
to fight, no power,
no eyes to guide us
no strength to oppose
            the forces
that kept us apart.

Naive and innocent
the world fell upon us
            ripped us
from the same womb
and tore asunder
the sacred bond
            of family

It did not come easy
we faced a common enemy
disunited and spiteful

before sweet womanhood
came to us, we gave up

I would like to hold
my sister
feel her warm embrace
and touch her spirit
just one time.

Gord

I hear music in the trees
I hear a song on the wind

I feel the moving power of stone
the strength of green mountains

The rain is the home
of my wandering spirit

Listen for me in the soft murmur
of the rivers and the rain

Do not weep
for I did not die

I do not sleep
I can see you
in your dark moments
I live next you

Call me
I will come

I bequeath my loyalty
the songs and love of the ageds

the spirit of our grandfathers
the heart of our grandmothers

Ah, but Gord you left too soon
too soon for me to tell you

I tried hard not to be resentful

at the compassion you held
for all people, and I admit

It was hard to love you
and know you held us no dearer
than the white rebels of this land

I confess I am not like you

I cannot always be gentle
am not always warm
impatience dogs my spirit
apathy plagues my life

Pillage

I rise each day watch sun
chase cloud 'cross dull, grey skies

witness rolling wood carry white 'cross my land
see railroad tracks laid by Chinese hands

"clear the trees
kill the buffalo
plunder the fish!"

Watch dead-wood buildings grow

Indian cotton, Chinese silk
fruit of African lands

"flood the country
with the pillage
of enslaved hands"

Bleed the children of dark humanity

Cedar tears
and buffalo grief
stain my face

My besieged grandchildren know not why.

Actress

(Nilak Butler)

I am an actress
                    a good one.

I have smiled
a thousand times
at people I have never met.

I am an image
I have held my head up
under circumstances
t'would shame a rose.

I can dramatize for you
the suffering of the multitudes
while my own dreams go unnoticed

I can act out for you
the pain of imprisonment
while my own pain
stays locked up.

Don't think me insensitive
I hear the whisperings,
"pst . . . she was an actor . . .
you know."

◇

Ah, behold the dramatist
that I struggle to be
yet cannot.

. . . that I could dramatize
our struggle, personify
each victory . . .
make real each step.

. . . that I could bury
my own pain
let my dreams fall to naught
that I could hide
my private agony
yet portray another's . . .

I would know how it is
to be you, NILAK
nay, more.
I would be an actress.

I could go to the big house
and immortalize
our story in dance.
you know.

Ancestors

Bent, bleeding bodies burnt brown by the sun in sugar-beet
fields,
tear toxic sweet from earth's bosom for childly consumption.

Cracked cold hands cut, swimmer, spilling guts and snapping
heads
from ocean's bounty to rot on concrete, cannery decks.

From my brother's chain-saw comes a screaming massacre for
lordly cedar,
to perish in the interest of profit.

Lest I learn, enemy of mine, pay me with alcohol, drug me,
lest I hear the ancient call of my ancestors—to arms?

On World Peace

The price of World Peace
is paid in human sacrifice.
The sacrifice of the interests
of the few for the benefit of all.

It requires unity
not just among the citizens
of this nation but unity
among the people of the world.

Vancouver Sath

Different Age Same Cage

(left to right) Jagdish Binning, Harjinder Sangra, Anju Hundal, Pindy Gill. *photo: Val Speidel*

Written and performed by an all-woman cast from Vancouver Sath. Written by Harjinder Sangra, Jagdish Binning and Anju Hundal. Performed as follows:

SANTOSH, the wife:	Pindy Gill
SURINDER, the husband:	Jagdish Binning
MOTHER:	Anju Hundal

SANTOSH: I wonder why Mom is not home yet? I'm going to have to leave for work soon.

SURINDER: She is usually home by this time.

SANTOSH: You can never tell what time she is going to get home.

SURINDER: Farmworkers don't work nine to five.

SANTOSH: They phoned again today.

SURINDER: Who phoned again?

SANTOSH: I told them to call tonight to talk to you. They want the suite by next week.

SURINDER: Look we've gone over this many times already. We can't give it to them.

SANTOSH: I hope you know where the money is coming from. The mortgage payment is due at the end of the month.

SURINDER: My UIC cheque should be here and you will get paid, we'll manage somehow.

SANTOSH: I don't think so. Have you forgotten about the property tax and car insurance? It's due next month you know.

SURINDER: So what do you suggest—I should throw my mother out of the house?

SANTOSH: I am not saying that, but we have to think of something.

SURINDER: I'll take care of it. You are giving me a headache. Aren't you late for work?

SANTOSH: (*looks at her watch and remembers*) Oh my god I am late! Where is she?

SURINDER: Why are you waiting for her?

SANTOSH: I have to tell her a few things about the kids. I also have to ask her if she can go to the gurudwara tomorrow to help make ladoos for my cousin's marriage.

SURINDER: Who is going to do all these things for you if we send her to live in the cabins on the farm?

SANTOSH: We managed before when she was in India.

SURINDER: We had only one kid then not four, remember?

SANTOSH: You can look after the kids now. Your mill is not going to start again.

SURINDER: Must we send her to the cabins?

SANTOSH: We can't put her in the bedroom upstairs with the kids. There is no room as it is.

SURINDER: I still don't feel right about it.

SANTOSH: You think I like it? We really need that five hundred dollars that we'll get from the basement suite.

SURINDER: I don't want to talk about it anymore, God damn it.

SANTOSH: Well you do what you please. They are going to call tonight. They're really interested in the place. Their kids go to the nearby school. They might even pay more than five hundred.

(MOTHER *enters*)

SANTOSH: I'm glad you're finally home. I have to go to work an hour early today. I've made some daal but you'll have to make rotis. Jeevan is going to be home around six o'clock, but he won't want roti for dinner. Make him a hamburger. Jesse is sleeping, her baby food is in the fridge, just heat it up a little. But make sure Deepi eats roti with her father. Don't make her anything else. And don't forget to give Jesse her cough medicine or it'll get worse.

SURINDER: Let her at least sit down.

SANTOSH: I wish I had time to sit down. (*she starts to leave, comes back*) Oh, Debo auntie phoned. They are going to make ladoos tomorrow. I can't go so you have to go, you are not working tomorrow, right? (*she leaves*)

MOTHER: (*shaking her head*) This wife of yours. I can't understand her, she runs around as if her pigtail is on fire. She never makes any sense to me. If your father was alive he would have laughed his head off.

SURINDER: She is OK Mom.

MOTHER: She may look OK to you. I think she has a few screws loose.

SURINDER: Yeah, sometimes she does act that way. Isn't she like that old Brahmin woman that used to come to our house and talk to grandmother for hours? Remember how we kids used to make fun of her.

MOTHER: She is a bit like her. Kesro had a good heart, she must have gone to heaven, poor soul. You still remember her, hey?

SURINDER: You don't forget things like that, Mom. (*senses her getting sentimental and tries to change the subject*) Make some roti, Mom, before little Jesse gets up.

MOTHER: No letter from India today? It's been so long since your auntie sent a letter. I hope everything is OK.

SURINDER: No letters today.

MOTHER: I miss everybody. I'd like to go back to India.

SURINDER: You don't want to go there now. Someone will probably kill you just for your money. Don't think too much about back home, just stay put, you're better off here working in the farms.

MOTHER: I should go in the winter.

SURINDER: Mom, it's a little tough for us now. Go when things get a bit easier. Anyway if you go in winter you won't get your UIC and that'll be really hard on the family. There are so many bills to pay. Things will be better soon financially, I promise, and then you can go.

MOTHER: That will be the day. You have been saying that for years. Some things never change. (*angrily*) I work thirteen to fourteen hours a day, come home, babysit, do chores for your stupid wife, make all the meals. I barely get a day off.

SURINDER: You think you're the only one with problems.

MOTHER: I don't know about others. All I know is that I never get any rest. That contractor treats us like animals, stuffing twenty of us like pigs in that small broken down van. You can't breathe in there, you can't straighten your legs for hours after. It is so exhausting.

SURINDER: Stop complaining, Mom.

MOTHER: I am not complaining. I have seen harder times in my life. I have never been afraid of work. It is just that I thought things would be different here in Canada.

SURINDER: Maybe you should live in the cabins there. That will make things easier for you.

MOTHER: Son, who will look after the kids here? There is so much to do—feeding the kids, washing clothes, giving them baths, making your roti, cleaning the rooms . . .

SURINDER: Don't worry about all that. Now that I'm laid off I can manage things.

MOTHER: No, Son, I don't want to go live in the cabins. I don't know anybody there.

SURINDER: But you wanted to go and live there last year.

MOTHER: That's because I knew Gurdev Kaur who was living in the cabins. Besides those cabins are so filthy. The new owner doesn't clean them. I wouldn't go there anyway. You need me, your kids need me. Who'll make your dinner? Who'll look after the kids when Santosh is at work?

SURINDER: We'll manage.

MOTHER: What is going on? Why are you in such a big hurry to get rid of me all of a sudden?

SURINDER: What do you mean? Who is trying to get rid of you? I only mentioned this because you were complaining about the contractor's van.

MOTHER: Don't try to hide things from me. I know there is something going on here. You guys were talking about getting five hundred dollars or something? What was that all about? Is it Santosh? Does she want me out of here?

SURINDER: Mom, there you go again, making a mountain out of

a mole hill! There is nothing going on. It's just that . . .

MOTHER: Just what? Go on, why have you stopped?

SURINDER: See, Mom, we thought that . . .

MOTHER: I'm listening.

SURINDER: See, we are already behind one month on the house payment, then there's the car insurance and a handful of other bills. I don't know how we're gonna manage it.

MOTHER: But why do you want to send me to the cabins?

SURINDER: Well you see, some people have been asking about renting the basement. They're willing to pay more than five hundred dollars a month. It will really help us get back on our feet.

MOTHER: So that is it, hey? Now you want to kick me out of the house? A fine son you are! They told me people change in Canada. But I never thought my own son would turn out to be like this.

SURINDER: (*angrily*) How can you say that, Mom? I'm not your enemy. I brought you here. I didn't even want you to work in the farms. You have been here eight years and this is only your second year in the farm.

MOTHER: Save it. I'm not used to such sneaky and conniving talk. You know it and I know it. You needed me to look after the kids then. The minute they were old enough, out I went to the farms.

SURINDER: Oh come on, Mom.

MOTHER: Don't mom me. I know your kind. You kids of this day and age have no guts left. I have lived through things that you can't imagine. We were never rich. Always had to struggle but we were a family and faced hardships together.

SURINDER: You can't expect us to do things the way you used to do. Things are different here.

MOTHER: Don't I know it. Are they ever different. You need a babysitter, use your mother; you need extra money, send your mother to work in the farms. You get behind on your payments, send her to live in the cabins. You don't see me as your mother, you see me as a slave that you can use anywhere.

SURINDER: You're really blowing things out of proportion. It is not that you are going to live there forever. It is only for a few months and then you can go to India.

MOTHER: I have heard that song before. Don't you worry about me. I can look after myself. Living in cabins won't kill me but if you don't get your money it might kill you. So you go ahead and rent your basement and get your lousy five hundred dollars.

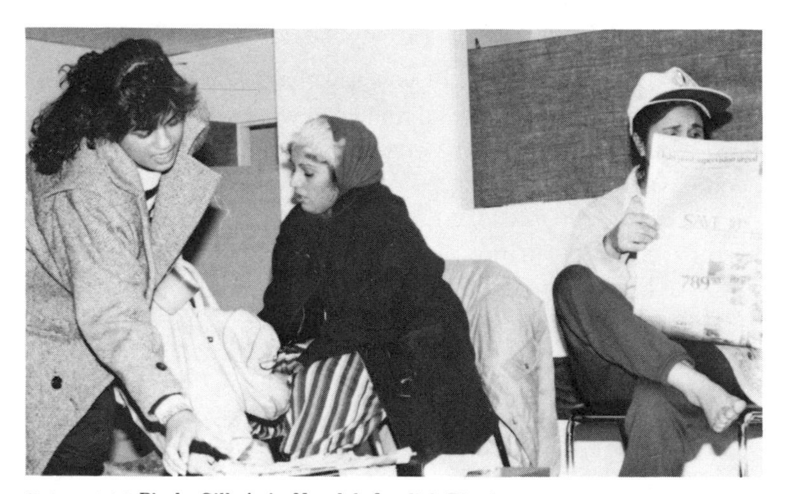

(*left to right*) Pindy Gill, Anju Hundal, Jagdish Binning. *photo: Evelyn Fingarson*

PANEL TWO

The Writer's Role in the Community

Panelists:
Joy Kogawa
Barbara Herringer
Sky Lee
Louise Profeit-LeBlanc

How do you sustain a different spiritual or political legacy?
What is the relationship of the writer to her audience?
How do you reconcile the call to political action with the call to write?

From the Bottom of the Well, From the Distant Stars

Joy Kogawa

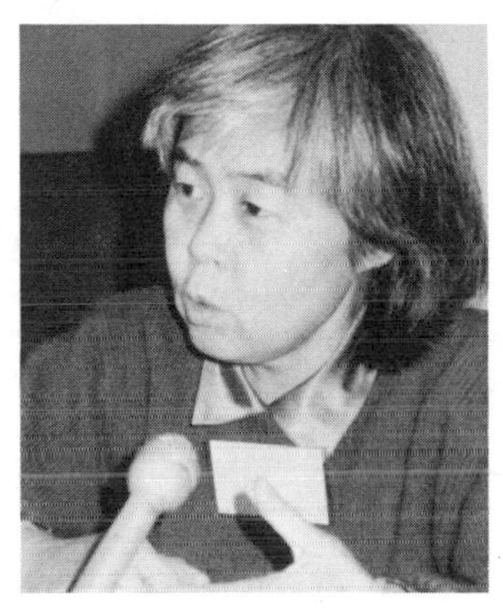

photo: Evelyn Fingarson

It's great to be here, and terrific to see you, Dorothy [Livesay]. I'd like to ask my dad [Canon Gordon Nakayama] to stand up. He just turned eighty-eight, and we had this great birthday party for him. I feel warm being here, seeing your faces, and I feel this is an inspiring community.

If you're a writer, and you're in a community of people that inspires you, then you're gonna write about that community. You're full of idealism and struggle. I have been involved in a community that has inspired me, and I think writers are very fortunate when they either come out of, or come into, or belong to, in some way, such a community. A writer can be inspired by a community and a community can also be uninspiring. You can choose, out of the panorama of human beings to be inspired if you so wish, because life is a great big banquet table, full of all kinds of good stuff to eat and it's got poison on it too. If you want to choose the rotten stuff on that table, you can do it. And I know it's here too.

I mean, the closer you get to any community, the more of the back alleys you can see, the more of the rotten stuff you can see. So you can choose to look at that, or you can choose to back up a little, and see the part that moves you, that touches you with its beauty, because a certain distance is often required.

Anyway, what I said when I was invited to come here was that I was not going to think about what I was going to say, because if I did that, I was going to have to stop writing, and I wouldn't be able to do what a writer is supposed to do, which is to write, not to speak.

In the novel that I'm writing right now, a sequel to *Obasan*, Aunt Emily is in Toronto, and there is a flashback to the fifties. Naomi gets drawn into a political struggle. She is a completely non-political type of person. She stays underground, she's subterranean; her stream of consciousness remains underground. Whereas Aunt Emily tromps on the earth. If a tree falls in her forest, everybody sees it. Aunt Emily says in one chapter, that art is the arena of the shadow warrior, of the shadow boxer of the soft shoe. She believes that politics is the sacrifice of the voice from the stars, but one of the other people argues that there are stars reflected in the well's dark bottom, and the voice from there also calls. And so, the artist and the political person cannot be differentiated in that sense.

What matters is that you listen to the voice that calls you, whether it comes from the bottom of the well, or whether it comes from the distant stars, whether it comes from your community, whether it comes from within your own heart, whether it comes from your neighbour or from your mate, or whomever it comes from, your calling is to respond to the voice that calls you. Fundamentally, that response is the response of love, so the writer's role is no different than any other human being's role, which is fundamentally to love and to respond to the voice that cries out to you. And Emily does that, and she sacrifices her writing for that.

I know that during the time when I wasn't writing because I was so involved with the community, I kept asking myself, "Is this what I'm supposed to be doing?" I've never really known, and I don't think we ever absolutely know whether we're doing the right thing or not. We just sort of stumble to the right, and we stumble to the left, and we struggle, and that's what it means to be part of the human condition. Somehow, it doesn't matter as long as you are listening to love's voice. So I guess that's all I've got to say for the moment.

For the Sounds of our Bodies

Barbara Herringer

photo: Evelyn Fingarson

I'd like to dedicate my little spiel to the women who haven't had the opportunity to "tell it," and particularly—from my point of view—lesbian women. These days I've been writing for different communities and for different audiences. The writing I do for love and for my own need is poetry, which is simmering and, like Joy's, hasn't had a whole lot of time to get out there, because I've been writing all sorts of other things. I'm doing technical writing for various social service agencies and I'm also trying to finish a thesis. But most of the writing, regardless of the genre, is for women, because in my experience there aren't a lot of men, whether they be social workers or poets, who are interested in women's lives or at least interested enough to ask us questions.

To be heard in our community, our community of women, we tell our stories. A lot of us experienced that this morning in Betsy and Louise's workshop; that's what we did, we told our stories. We listen to stories, we talk about other women's stories and we gossip, basically. We tell our bodies. Our lives are political: we're the body politic. That phrase seems perfect for women.

One day, when I was about four, my mother asked me what I wanted to be when I grew up and I answered "God." Later I think I wanted to be a nurse but being God was really my great ambition. The omnipotence of a supreme being really appealed to me back then and in some ways it still does. I want to change the world. I tried to do that years ago—I'm an ex-nun. Ten years ago though, I discovered my body for the first time, by making love with another woman and, believe me, that really changed the landscape and my mother tongue, especially when I began calling myself by one of the world's most feared words, which is "lesbian."

I remember times then, which are unfortunately infrequent these days, when I would write all night long in an attempt to name or tell or locate who I was with that change. And I kept coming back to the old father language, the God language I had grown up with, and I couldn't find it. Writing as a lesbian is making what other people call the "forbidden," visible. It's exploding the language that I grew up with—transforming it too, into mother tongue. Mother tongue is a familiar place to a lot of us, but it's a very dangerous place when we really start speaking it out there in the world.

One of the things that angered me most, and still does actually, is that when I began to uncover the layers of what it meant for me to call myself a lesbian ten years ago (and believe me I struggled over that word too, having grown up Catholic) was what it meant in the eyes of society. Not just that vague old society out there, but my mother, my brothers, my friends. It didn't matter what I had done in the past, what jobs I had held, what things I had done—all of a sudden I was who I slept with. And I found that hard.

When I first started to uncover myself in that way, I was dismissed because of my body and I think that's a measure of the threat that we face. We are with and for women; consequently, as lesbian women, we lose our children, lose our jobs, lose our housing, and lose our lives. We're not allowed to participate in communal ritual or religion. We're asked to leave convents and, along with our gay brothers, we are not allowed to minister in most churches. When lesbians speak of our lives others flinch and get kind of "creepy" or else they get angry. Why do you have to call yourself a lesbian writer? Why do you have to call yourself a lesbian social worker, or a lesbian anything: why do you have to say anything at all? Well, that's my core.

I was rereading some poetry the other day and came across a piece by Black poet Claire Harris. In the statement she was making she said, I am a Black poet: any poetry I write is Black poetry. And I say, I'm a Lesbian poet and any poetry I write is Lesbian poetry. I write from that core, that place that's mine, so that I'm not invisible. There are risks with that and some of us stay hidden. Some of us stay hidden by ourselves or along with our lover; we pass, you wouldn't recognize us. We write about anything but ourselves, the way a lot of women poets do and have done in the past; write in the male voice without even thinking about it, assuming "he," because he is universal—"she" doesn't exist. We're all human, they say, well yeah, OK, we are, but we're also beings with differences that need to be acknowledged and that really cry out to be celebrated.

Believe it or not, all lesbians are not the same. We are of varying classes, races, ethnic backgrounds and as Jeannette said yesterday, "sizes," and ages. Some of us are mothers or aunties or spinsters or celibate, some of us are sexual, monogamous: call them A and call them B, we're not the same. Not all lesbians are feminists, not all lesbians like women, not all lesbians call themselves lesbians. There is one thing we share though, in all this, and that's an oppression. That oppression—from family, from our friends, from the church, from the state, from the legal profession, from the educational system, from other women, from the women's community—is homophobia. And although it's slowly changing, we're also invisible in the cultural mainstream and our work is all too frequently greeted with silence. Often we must publish our own work, establish our own journals, newsletters, galleries, and networks. But we are telling it and our work and the work of other women here today is challenging that dominant culture.

It's interesting, I was flipping through the dictionary again just to find out for myself, now what do they mean by culture? We're always talking about Canadian culture, and how it's going to be lost with Free Trade and so on. Anyway, Webster's defines culture as "the total pattern of human behavior and its product, embodied in thought, speech, action and artifacts and dependent on man's capacity for learning and transmitting knowledge to succeeding generations through the use of tools, language and systems of abstract thought. Culture is the body of customary beliefs, social forms and material traits constituting a distinct complex of tradition of a racial, religious or social group." My feeling is that any woman speaking out and placing her foot firmly on the earth is reworking that definition for herself and her community. Lesbian writers could name ourselves as community workers, writing for social change, living as community organizers, moving and organizing with other women for radical change—radical meaning of the roots or going to the roots; essential to life or primary.

As radicals, we write for ourselves and our community: for the community which has the courage to hear us, not burn us; for the community eager to hear another voice, another culture, another country. We write for the sounds of our bodies, for the words our tongues create; we write because to speak of our lives is a political act and to be silent is to keep other women silent as well. We write as lesbians. We are telling it. Nicole

Brossard says, “a lesbian who does not re-invent the world is a lesbian in the process of disappearing.”

Women In Touch Coming Home

Sky Lee

photo: Jacqueline Frewin

It's really wonderful to see so many women here. I have a good friend, May Lynn Woo. Once May Lynn tried to analyze me, and she told me about people—people in their gardens, and how they cultivate their little private gardens, hopefully towards an emotional stability which will sustain them. Some people don't have private gardens; they have collective plots, perhaps because they are in a collective struggle. But either way, we all cultivate our gardens—some better than others, some not so good, but all with the hope that it will nourish us back one day. May Lynn told me that my garden has been cultivated to perfection. The walls around it are sound, and it is a very private garden.

Recently, thanks to a new friend, a poet named Jean Yoon, I discovered an Asian American writer, Hisaye Yanamoto, who wrote this passage in her book of short stories, entitled *Seventeen Syllables.* It's about an obscene phone call. I thought it was a reply of sorts to May Lynn, and also a way to address this panel. I like it because it's not a very pat answer or solution—

not that any of us are looking for pat answers.

> Whatever, whatever. I knew I had discovered yet another circle to put away with my collection of circles. I was back to what I started with, the helpless, absolutely useless knowledge that the days and nights must surely be bleak for a man who knew the compulsion to thumb through the telephone directory for a woman's name, any woman's name; that this bleakness, multiplied infinite times (see almost any daily paper) was a great, dark sickness on the earth that no amount of pansies, pinks or amaryllis, thriving joyously in what garden however well-ordered and pointed to with pride, could ever hope to assuage.[1]

I love that image of a woman interrupted, dug out of her flower garden, called to answer all the obscene phone calls this world has to offer. I often feel like that. I'm a private person; I'm not used to public speaking. I rebelled at first. So, what apparently gave me, not the right—everybody has the right—but the righteousness to speak on the writer's role in the community. Oh, we discussed it very thoroughly at our next Asian women's group.

May Lynn started off indignantly, "It's the writing, not the writer that has a role in the community. The writer gets ego-identified with the writing, so the role of writers is seen as greater than what it really is."

Lorraine Chan said, "If writing is to have a role, it would be like a soap-opera, and allow people to emote while escaping their own realities."

May Lynn said, "Creative writing just pushes the boundaries of reality back a bit."

Lorraine said, "Writing will empower the Chinese-Canadian community by reflecting our history, and our culture. It must have resonance with our community, but must also deal with the marketplace."

May Lynn said, "Books reflect the consumerist instincts of our society. People don't want to engage in the creative process; we just want to consume."

I said, "It's not easy to streamline 3-dimensional reality, 4-dimensional fantasy, multi-fractional psychotic episodes into tiny black words on white blank paper."

May Lynn said, "So we deify the producer to avoid the responsibility of going through the same things ourselves."

Lorraine said, "Just tell them you need to get published to sustain our different political and spiritual legacy."

May Lynn concluded, "The question is meant to puff up the role of the writer . . . "

"But," I said, "to the writers who have gone through the process, we don't need that, do we?" And as a writer who has gone through the process in my own little way, I can only invite anyone who wants to come, into my garden. And we can talk about living in a garden, within or without the context of that world out there. We can talk about the garden as home, a room of her own, a guerrilla base, or the garden as her identity, her inner well-being, her taking back of her own sexuality.

As a writer who has gone through the process in my own little way, with the words of Judy Radul, Vancouver poet, from her *Rotating Bodies*, I can say, "I am only a voice."[2]

What dare I know of anyone's role in the community? And imagine Judy's audacity when she also said, "The voice is always in context, because it remakes itself for every space."

However, my voice here does get stronger, because there are women listening here and elsewhere. These women I love and care about, and I want to tell them that I have a vested interest in writing about them. They are part of my community, your community; they are part of many circles, magnified infinite times.

As a writer, I can share a secret. Viola and I were skimming over northern B.C. waters, when we created a code for witch—"Women In Touch Coming Home." I don't need to define you, you know who you are. It's real important to me that beauty like ours survive, not only survive, but get free, and grow. We are the ones who are in battle to survive. It's a lifelong marathon, and it's tiring and it's sad. We are in danger of drowning in despair because there's no tangible hope in sight yet. Our very identities as women stripped down to the ugliest of sexual words. You know this as well as I. If we own anything at all, it's faith, faith in our own life-creating forces, faith in our healing.

As a writer who has gone through the process in my own little way, I want to give you words of encouragement. Too many of us have lost touch and are battering ourselves against a wall. In battles, there is a waxing and a waning too. Mao once wrote on the importance of guerrilla bases in extended warfare:

> the circumstances are often such as to make it necessary to run away. The ability to run away is precisely one of the characteristics of the guerrilla; running away is the chief means of getting out of passivity and regaining the initiative.[3]

My guerrilla base is my garden, where I escape to rest. Come home to your garden, your collective plot, someone else's garden; just get in touch again! To heal is often the hardest thing to do, especially when we've gotten so used to being ill or injured. It is a way of fighting for our humanness. This vision of a woman in her garden is to me a very important one. Ultimately, the vision of a woman tilling and cultivating her garden called earth is the only one I want to pass on unsullied to my great granddaughters. Remember, Mao only went a little ways with his revolution. Now as women, we must regain the initiative and go much much farther. We must go where no man has gone before.

Sources

1. Hisaye Yanamoto, *Seventeen Syllables* (Latham NY: Kitchen Table, Women of Color Press, 1988).
2. Judy Radul and Carel Moiseiwitsch, *Rotating Bodies: Alexis, Crystal, Blake* (Vancouver, B.C.: Petarade Press, 1988).
3. Anne Fremantle, ed., *Mao Tse-Tung, An Anthology of His Writing* (New York NY: Mentor Books, 1962).

Ancient Stories, Spiritual Legacies

Louise Profeit-LeBlanc

photo: Evelyn Fingarson

I don't call myself a writer, I call myself a speaker. One of the most significant things in my own development was something my elders taught me. They have always said, "When you're speaking to people you must remember you're an instrument; remember there are many hearts there, they are all in different places and you might be in another place." If we speak and there are elders among us, we must be very careful how we choose our words. I feel very honored that this elderly gentleman* is sitting here in front.

My grandmother appointed a very special woman, Lucy Cho, to be my spiritual mentor. Lucy Cho took me aside one day, during the time I was involved in a political Indian organization in the Yukon. I was very tired at the time and she said, "You know what your problem is?" "No, please tell me," I answered. She said, "You don't open your meetings with a

---

*Canon Gordon Nakayama, Joy Kogawa's father.

prayer and you people don't handle your business in a spiritual way, and from now until the end you will suffer from that." So, I want to begin this with a little prayer in my own language. [. . .] That's for her.

When I first looked at this title, it seemed scary. It says, "How do you sustain a different spiritual or political legacy?" I live it. My daughter was five-and-a-half years old when I sent her to kindergarten. I remember the day she came home with real happiness on her face. She flipped open her little book and she said, "Mom, see that? It's talking to me." I can't tell you the joy I felt because in that one little sentence, in that one little shared thought of my daughter with myself, I traversed centuries, thousands of years of history of my people not writing down these little black squiggles.

I have been nourished by a community that is so vocal, so open, so giving, so rich in oral tradition that we can share stories told from a perspective that is 30,000 years old. Everything from the land exudes stories. Everything. The stones tell stories. If you travel with an elder, they have a story to tell.

There is a beautiful lake near my home community. It's called Kwan Mun or Ta Kwan Da Mun. The English name is Ethel Lake. How sad. I think some surveyor named it after his Aunt Ethel, which was a dignified thing to do, but nobody in the Yukon knows Ethel. In the new name the old story is lost. At one point in the history of the development of the northern Tutchone people they fished there with lit torches on the edge of the lake and afterward they had a big party. Kwan means Fire, Mun means lake, Ta Kwan Da Mun: Firelake, the place of the big party. This is the place where they hung their furs and invited the people of the other villages to come to them to have a potlatch and enjoy the ritual of contest to see who was the strongest or who could drink the most grease. That may sound grotesque to you, but that is what happened. It was how these chiefs and powerful people expressed their strength. I am sorry to say today, to you people, that Kwan Da Mun has been graded away and it's a campground.

I and a friend went down there and did a surface search—archaeological work; I am interested in that. We came across surface finds right on the lake, lots of points, arrowheads "they" call them. All kinds of activity there. My people hung out there. All the trees there know the story of the people. They suffered with the people when the fish were not plentiful. They rejoiced in the birthing of new babies, the people coming in with meat, the harvesting of the land and the great sharing of stories.

When I was invited to this conference, I thought, "Great, now I can tell some of the stories nobody else has heard." I am sure you here have been in touch with your grandparents. You know how special that is. I want to tell you the story of Good Woman. It is very old. (Maybe some day some archaeologists will tell me how old it is. We had no way of knowing exactly how to put incidents and stories in touch with how many years ago they happened). I think it's really important as a person raised in my community by grandparents to share stories and to help get rid of a stereotype view of my people.

We didn't always live in comfort as some believe. We suffered from the elements: we starved, some of us froze, some of us drowned, all kinds of tragedies occurred. Despite all the tragedies, we lived a happy life. One of the elders in a northern community said, "You know what the best thing to do for your people and your community is? Be happy. You," he said, "you're a happymaker, that's your job." I pay homage to the gentleman who gave me this story. He gave it to me at a time when I was really struggling to find a rhyme and a reason why we do things, to understand why we don't just sit down and start writing some of our heartfelt feelings. Sometimes I feel as if we neglect our-self. To him, to his mother who told him, and to her mother who told her, I pay homage.

This occurred at a time of great starvation in the Yukon. Winter had come too soon. The berries froze, the people were not able to get as much food as they usually did. The caribou had taken another trail that year, quite a ways from where they were camped, so they didn't have much meat. They had some fish, but not enough.

This old couple were out on the land by themselves. She was barren, so they didn't have any kids to take care of them. Every morning they'd get up together, they'd pray to get something and then, he'd go out. He returned day after day, empty-handed, but still they repeated the process never losing heart. Their hunger grew.

This day, she is in the initial stages of starvation, emaciated and skinny, eyes sunk in. Now in the Yukon Territory there is a special relationship between a little bird called a whiskey jack, some people call him camp robber, and the moose. This little bird has a very strong power over moose. (Indian term: deecho). The old people know you're going to find moose when that little camp robber comes around and talks to you. He says, "See that? . . . Gimme fat . . . I want moose fat." Anyway, this old man he went out this one morning. He was really getting destitute. He thought, "My gawd, I have to do something for my wife." It's very barren there, lots of snow and the trees are not very tall, maybe four or five feet. The only thing he saw out there was a little whiskey jack.

He had a very difficult time deciding what to do, but in the end he killed the bird and took it home. He emptied it out on the place where he and his wife were living. She prepared the bird for cooking. She boiled it up and drank a little bit of the soup. You know when you are really hungry and you eat, you get full fast, so it's not good to eat lots when you are starving. That woman said, "Let's save these two little drumsticks. Put them over here, until tomorrow." "OK," he said. They went to sleep that night and the next morning they got up early. He's going to go out again. This time he felt determined to bring something back. Just before he leaves she says, "Just a minute. You better have one of these drumsticks. Here, take one for the trail." "No," he said, "you eat it, you need it more than me." "No," she said, "you take it." He left. Didn't take it. It wasn't too far from his camp and he saw a moose calf and a cow, right there. He killed both of them with his arrow. Boy, you really give thanks, eh, cutting it up? He took the special parts, kidney, liver and heart out. It's what we eat first back home. He couldn't carry lots of meat, too weak, so he put those special parts in his packsack and brought it home. He and his wife started to prepare the food—gonna eat it. "Just a minute," she said, "Hold on there." She went and got those drumsticks . . . "Let's eat these first."

That is the story of Good Woman. For a long time we put those drumsticks away. Now is our time to tell it. Don't be silent anymore, but at the same time there is strength in silence. That's why we have two ears and one mouth. We must listen, not just with our ears, but with our hearts. We have to train those thoughts in our heads to stop talking, get real quiet inside, and listen to each other and unite with everybody in our community in order to make it a better place to live.

That's why I try to make these stories receivable, not only by my own people—although they are my most important audience—but by people at large, so they can have a glimpse of understanding. (You can never fully understand).

The beauty of these conferences, especially writers' conferences, is that while we are just sitting here enjoying this wonderful banquet of ideas, we get new ideas ourselves. Like lightbulbs. I want to end this presentation with a lightbulb I received here. It came to me in terms of my relationship with the birds, animals and bugs... Sometimes I forget about my little brothers and sisters there. I have to respect them too.

Spiders in training
Don't step on them.
The power they contain,
My Dahling... they will bring the rains.

Panel Two: Audience Discussion

(*left to right*) Viola Thomas, Joy Kogawa, Louise Profeit-LeBlanc, Sky Lee, Barbara Herringer. *photo: Evelyn Fingarson*

DOROTHY LIVESAY: This has been a wonderful experience for me. I think we are here, all of us, as part of a minority. Many minorities are here, and it's going to be hard always to accept a very different minority from our own. In my case I represent a group that's probably not here at all, the androgyne, the bisexual, and I just wonder to what degree this group, particularly Barbara perhaps, respects and understands a person who is built that way.

BARBARA HERRINGER: Do you really want me to answer that one, Dorothy? (*laughter*) I think I can respect that position quite well because I have also been with men more in my life than I have been with women, up until this point. In describing my own process, the only thing that I can say is that it has been more—and I'm speaking personally now—more of an *emotional* commitment to women over the years. I think that a lot of people have a fantasy about who we are as lesbians and, for myself, I think that fantasy comes down to who we are sexually. I can't speak for anybody else in the room, but because of various personal stresses my sexual life right now is not that great. But there are a lot of *different ways* that we connect in our relationships.

ANONYMOUS: That's enough. I guess you explained everything. (*laughter*)

BETSY WARLAND [from the audience]: I'm torn in two different ways. I've been at a lot of literary gatherings over the years and this one has meant the most to me. I feel that probably in the depths of our hearts we long to feel that we do belong in all of our differences, that that's home somehow, and I've really felt more at home here than I have anywhere else. But I have a question about that that I would address to all of you: when do we know who our communities are?—and I think you all do, as far as you know who you're writing to. But in what ways can those communities sometimes raise the possibility of limits for us as writers and artists? Have you encountered that and if so what have you done with that?

JOY KOGAWA: Aunt Emily talks about the writer and the artist as a shadow boxer. People have expectations and demand your time, and when you withdraw, you're labelled a betrayer. If you hurt somebody you respond and that takes away your time and you can't write. So my response has been to give up my writing, which labels me a betrayer in another way. I've done that for a time, and what Aunt Emily says is that sometimes you have to make that choice. If somebody's drowning close by, you don't listen to the voice from the stars, you listen to that immediate voice beside you and you respond to it and that's not to be seen as a limitation, it's to be seen as the moment of choice. What I feel is that life will give you time: if you're supposed to write, you'll write when you can. I'm hoping that the time when I can write is here now. You know, the community has gone through one struggle—life is an on-going struggle. I can continue to struggle, but the form of that struggle has changed. We always have the wolf blowing our walls down one way or another, and if you're going to stand there and defend your house or do what you've got to do, you need to define for yourself who the wolves are that you're supposed to be tackling, and sometimes it's a government, sometimes it's a sense of the enemy, sometimes it's just a shadow. You fight those in all different kinds of ways and I've been going through years of scratching the walls of my heart and my mind trying to define and name what my enemies are. Practically all my life I have not involved myself in political struggles. They seemed to be short term, just too immediate. I wanted to expend my energies on, you know, what it's going to be like at that moment of death, what about the unknown, what about that world that's just so much bigger than anything we can think of. I felt pulled to that exploration so I was very uninterested in the immediate things. I don't know quite how and when the changeover came but it seems to me to have been a gradual process that came after I had written *Obasan*. It came as a certain capacity to speak seemed to be coming forth, because I was in fact, if you've read *Obasan*, like Naomi, and she's very, very quiet. I was like that almost all my life, I couldn't even put my hand up to ask questions in class I was so shy. Now somewhere along the line I got pushed into having to speak and I would be so nervous and I would swear I would never do it again because it would be so horrible, but you do that often enough, sometimes you go beyond. There's a statement that's attributed to Jesus—I think it's written in the Gnostic Gospels, it's not in the Bible—but the statement that he was supposed to have made was, if you give birth to that which is within you, that which is within you will save you. If you do not give birth to that which is within you, that which is within you will destroy you. I think that when you are pushed to come out from that cocoon and make those tentative stumbling speeches and you keep doing it and doing it, eventually you break loose, break free, come into another world, and then you go on.

TIMMY TIMMS: What I'm going to say is for all the unpublished people, the failed writers, the silent people. I told someone this morning that I had been writing for over forty years and this is very true—with limited success, but I'm hard on myself. I find that women wear their themes like scarves. My theme for the past three or four months had been isolation. I had submitted three items to a federal literary competition and had seen two of them come home—"come home," isn't that nice? I had seen two of them come home on Monday, and I said oh my god, this possibly means that the third one is a success. It came home on Tuesday and my daughter happened to be there and I just cried and cried. I had been taking courses at Douglas College, I had been doing self-assertion, I had been doing anger, how to deal with criticism, and I still cried. But wearing this scarf of isolation, I was able to know that what I had entered was a kind of Olympics and I had entered it without a coach, without mentors, without any funding, so of course it would come back. I'm carrying this forward to all of us women here, that we should not enter any arena alone.

DAPHNE MARLATT: I want to pick up on Dorothy's courageous statement and ask a question about the negative effects of community. We've talked a lot about the positive effects, though Joy has talked about the negative effects in terms of the call to political action and how that can silence you as a writer. I'd like to hear from you about how the self-definition of a community can silence someone who doesn't feel included in that definition. For instance, there's been a lot of discussion in the lesbian community about whether bisexual women are to be included as really lesbian or not. Every community has a kind of grey area and each of us who speaks her difference moves into that grey area as soon as we speak out. I'd like to know how you have experienced that and how you deal with the silencing involved.

LOUISE PROFEIT–LEBLANC: I'd like to attempt to answer that question because at times people tried to silence me and particularly in the area of cedar. I want to share a real brief story with you that hits the nail right on the head and I share it with a lot of my friends, particularly in the Native community. There were two people and they were on the beach and they were catching crabs. I've never crabbed in my life so I just took it verbatim from this man from the West Coast who had crabbed. I was going through some struggles and I was telling him my problems and he said, I'll tell you a little story. He says, there were two guys crabbing on the beach and one kept having to push his crabs back in the pot and the other man just kept catching crabs and he didn't have to push his back in. Finally at the end of the day, the curiosity killed the cat of this other guy and he went over and he said, hey what kind of crabs are those? And he said, them's Indian crabs. What? He said, when one of them starts getting out the other ones pull him back down. So I can really relate to this question and, you know, once my voice started coming out of the little crabbing trap people wanted to pull me back down. I too can really relate to what Joy was saying, that once you break the silence and you realize your humanness, it doesn't matter what walk of life you come from if you have a joy to share, or lessons that you can share to help your community grow. I know that I was involved in a play—it was called *Raven at my Door* and you can call it "raving at my door" because that's basically what happened in the Native community and it was a very painful process, let me tell you. This particular play was written by a friend of mine, non-Indian, and she was in full consultation with quite a few Native people who are writers. She had the courage to give it to some Native actors and actresses and say redo it with the help of a producer and a director. She trusted that. It caused such havoc in the community I remember saying oh god nobody's going to show up for this play and I was taking part in it and, oh lordy, it caused such a stir. My own people wanted to boycott it because—and I sorted it out during the process—it was touching some truths. Now quite often when people put a mirror in front of you and tell you a truth, you don't want to look there because it hurts. So I'll tell you the positive end of a very negative beginning is that because of all this backlash we had all kinds of PR. People on the street would stop and say, what's this play? what's coming down? and I said, oh well this is a play, and I'd just give it to them how it was. I must tell you that that play brought out street people that would never come out to a theatre production. And one young man came to me—he's a reformed alcoholic and his wife is still battling with alcohol—and his comment alone made it all worthwhile. He said, you know that guy? That's me. So let's remember the crab story.

SKY LEE: Talking about how community can limit you and silence you—OK, take your example about being in the lesbian community, Daphne, with all these issues about being a lesbian these days. I remember there was a friend who said, I'd never agree to being a lesbian because these days you'd never know what you're agreeing to. What is a lesbian? Is it a political cause? Is it because you love women? Is it because you're having sex with women? I don't know. In the Western sense it is, you know, very sexually defined. Now I'd like to tell you about my beliefs of the Eastern sense of being a lesbian. I'm a lesbian, but I'm also bisexual and I'm heterosexual, but I like to currently think myself a lesbian. On the issue of bisexuals being lesbian or not, I just can't imagine half the world not loving another half of the world because, I don't know, because they're lesbian or het. I just can't imagine that world, and I don't want to believe in it. But in an Eastern sense, a women's community is very interesting. Women love women in my sense of the Asian community, which has, as its source, the village where my mother came from. It was very hard for her to come to Canada here. It's because she came from a very loving women's community and into this really bleak Western alienation. But in the village she came from, there was a whole community of women living together, working together, loving each other and they could never appreciate that until they left it probably. Still, there was and is a lot of patriarchal control. Ultimately, women can love women as much as they want but marriage is like death, you can't escape it. You only escape it by suicide, literally, and that's the ultimate power of patriarchal control. But interestingly enough, in the Asian sense women are allowed to be women, left to play or work together, probably because the relationships between men and women are often more taboo—more rules about how you relate to your uncle than how you relate to another woman, because that's the kind of patriarchal control of women's bodies which is important. Still, in my mother's community, of course women love women. So what is a lesbian? Where is this Western sense of lesbianism coming from? It is very limiting, I mean, or it is, as you say, silencing.

JOY KOGAWA: We all have a multitude of identities foisted on us. I tried to deny my ethnic identity because of what this country decided to do with people of Japanese origin. I hardly knew any Japanese-Canadians until I got involved in the movement for redress. I think that when you struggle with an intentional community, you struggle from a base of ideals and that becomes the community that means a very great deal to you. Now it happened in the redress movement that two identities got meshed. It was an intentional community as well as an ethnic community and that made it quite powerful. But I don't know whether I will remain there. So we're talking—I mean, Daphne, you were talking about the grey area. For me the grey areas occur when I move out of one community into another community. It's not that these grey areas are limiting. They're liberating. An identity can be a hair coat. If I can take off this painful thing and put on another kind of coat for a while, I can feel a lot freer. I don't want to be defined by and limited by any singular identity. I would like to be able to move as fluidly as possible, and the more I can move, the greater the sense of freedom and flight in the sense of being able to fly. I haven't been in a women's group for a long time because I've been involved in a Japanese-Canadian group, and I feel free at this moment just to be here and to feel a sense of identity with the struggle of women. I feel liberated from the hair coat of ethnicity that I've been having to wear recently. It's been painful. To me this is much more joyful. I know if I were in the heart of this struggle and wearing it in the way that some of you wear it, it wouldn't be a joyful coat only, it would be a very painful one. And I know that that's what one's garment becomes when you are tightly encased in it. It can become a carapace, you know, you can be unable to grow because you cannot move out of it. So I think it's important to be able to move out of one identity into another and to look for the core of why it is that you would choose to be in any single identity. I don't want to stay within my ethnic community if it's not involved in a love struggle of some kind. I would rather move over to something that is going to say something more to the world. Because I know as a kid I wanted to change the world, I wanted to be involved in some kind of forefront movement to make the world a better place, and I suppose the change happens from within many movements. And all of us together, feeling the pain and the joy and the interchangingness of the struggles, form a strong bond and reinforce each other. When we exercise our imaginations this way, we can also assist one another in braking loose from the pathology of choosing to be victims.

JEAN YOON: Joy, I was really glad to hear what you said about ethnicity becoming a carapace and being limiting because that's something I've found myself. If you are identified as belonging to any minority you are, as a writer, expected somehow to represent or be the mouthpiece for it, and that I think is how belonging to a community or feeling an identity or responsibility to a community can feel limiting. And Sky, I have a little problem with what you were saying about women's communities in the East because, having spent some time in Korea and China, the only time I ever heard a reference to lesbianism was in a conversation. My Korean wasn't so good and I was listening to it, going yeah? this is neat, and I'm nudging my friend who also was an English teacher there and she says, are they talking about what we *think* they're talking about? Yes, I think they're talking about what we think they're talking about. And of course they were talking about lesbianism but they weren't using a specific word for it. It was something that they couldn't even conceive of, and this was a group of women who were often talking and complaining about their men, but when it came down to the idea of actual sexual relations or of an exclusive relationship with women, there was absolutely no framework for that. So if you talk about community of women in Asia as an ideal, I think you have to be very careful because it's within a framework where the women are kept inside and there's no one else really to interact with. The way women relate to each other is very rigidly controlled. You can hold hands and stuff and spend all your time with your girlfriend but that's because there is absolutely no framework or possibility for escaping into another realm of relationships.

SKY LEE: Jean, just as you said, they have no sexual definition of lesbianism. They don't, you see. What I was trying to get across is that there is an idea of woman love and it's a little bit larger than lesbianism. I hear what you're saying, but what I'm saying is that in the face of that kind of oppression which you know exists in Asia and elsewhere, you also know that there are women coming together very intensely to fight it, right?

JEAN YOON: Can we talk about this later?

SKY LEE: (*laughter*) Sure, of course.

AUDIENCE: Now, now. (*more laughter*)

JEAN YOON: OK. To start, one thing within the Confucian system, which is what you'll see in China, in Korea and in Japan, though it's somewhat deconstructed in China, is that all relationships are hierarchical with men at the top and then it's also hierarchical by age. So relationships between women are very much regulated by age and you have to gauge who's older, who's more respectful, so that one of the most critical relationships between women in that system is the relationship between mother-in-law and daughter-in-law, which is an awful position to be in as a daughter-in-law. If you're on an equal basis, if you're with your peers, yes, there is a lot of freedom and the potential for intimacy and friendship is very strong. But I still believe that when you get women coming together and complaining about their men, their problems, their this and that, it's a commonality of grievance which has its usefulness and power, but on the other hand, it is, as well, a limitation, if that's the only level you connect on. If this woman-loving concept is one that arises because you're all in pain, then what happens when that pain is gone? It means you have to reassess the way you relate, and I don't think that that's fully developed in Asia right now. These are general ideas in my head. I just think it's very dangerous to make it an ideal because I don't think it's that simple.

SKY LEE: Ideals are never simple.

SILVA TENENBEIN: I don't consider the lesbian community, which I'm part of, confining at all. I'm delighted. I consider that I'm in the women's community by default, because I'm too belligerent to be anywhere else. And I think that's true of a lot of us, that we're here not because we want to be confined within the definition but because we don't fit within anybody's definition and we don't want to. One of the things that we do have in common is that we're forging new tools to make new definitions of ourselves and we're going to take that language and introduce it to the rest of the world.

JEANNETTE ARMSTRONG [from the audience]: I just want to thank the panel members for the things that they were saying and I want to maybe make a comment about the community. I had a little bit of a hard time with your story, Louise, and I guess what I'd like to say is that the guy didn't finish the story and I'd like to finish it if you'll let me. What he didn't tell you was that when the crab got pulled back down again he said, why are you pulling me back down? why don't you let me go? and the Indian crabs told him, well you're an Indian crab, you know better than to go up there and abandon us. Why don't you show us instead how you got up there? Why don't we work it out so we can all get up to the top instead of just you going? So that was how the story really was. And he said, yeah, you're right, get on my back first and the next guy get on his back and his back and his back, and when we get up to the top we'll all pull each other up and I'll make sure everybody gets up there before I do.

LOUISE PROFEIT-LEBLANC: Thank-you, Jeannette. I was just thinking, as you were telling me the ending, I just kind of felt like he hadn't finished the story. Not being from the West Coast, we have another story that's similar but it doesn't describe it in terms of the crabs. It's another story where you get back in there as much as the stew pot is really simmering and boiling and hurting and help each other swim to shore.

UNIDENTIFIED SPEAKER: The question raised about criticism and differences within communities is something I've been thinking about a lot lately. I'm an out lesbian in a pretty mainstream school system and what I hear, pretty well everywhere, is, isn't it awful how women put down other women? isn't it dreadful? look at that awful woman over there putting down other women. I think we often forget to put our energy where the problem is. The problem isn't the way we're all struggling to deal with our own oppression, the problem is our oppressor, the patriarchal system, and I think we often forget to point our energies *out* because we get very busy pointing them *in*. We're all struggling at different levels and everybody's at different places. I know that, for me, it's often very easy to be really hard on the woman who said that awful thought I might have just corrected in myself a week ago. It's sort of like being nouveau riche, it's nouveau consciousness-raised. I mean we have to keep educating each other with patience and with love and with our hearts. Those to me are hard words to say because they're Hallmark card words, but I think we need to take them back. And we need to keep our energies focused on who it is we're fighting, who it is we really need to educate.

SANDY SHREVE: A few years ago a friend of mine asked me a question about writing and the pressure I felt from the community. At that point I was writing primarily work poetry, poetry from the workplace, and she said, well do you ever feel scared? like, I can't say that, no, no, edit it out because my friends won't like it, it's not the way to think. And I said, no, never. Being in the union just keeps my grounded, you know, no problem. A few weeks later I was trying to write something and her words came back to me and I realized that I lied outright and it made me think a whole lot about some of those constrictions on writing that come from the community and it made me try to think about the balance. I get a lot of strength from the community where I work and live, and lots of inspiration, and I've always said if I didn't have that I couldn't write. It's also true, though, that during my activism in very far left-wing politics a number of years ago, I was always terrified of being wrong and I worked very hard to conform, to be, you know, the guiding light determined to change the world and get the answers, and I just couldn't stand it when I said something that sounded stupid or wasn't enlightened enough. So I have a whole history of that too. When I'm trying to write political kinds of things or things that maybe will contribute to change, I'm fighting between looking for what it is I really believe and worrying about whether other people will think I've betrayed the cause and trying to find the balance between being proscriptive and exploring. I saw a video a few days ago, about a woman called Pat Schultz and, at one point in the video, some lesbian women were talking with some heterosexual women and Pat Schultz, who was an older woman, was saying, I envy you all so much for your ability to begin to explore that side of your sexuality, I will never be able to. I grew up in this time, in this place, with these lessons and these strictures and I can't do it and I wish I were born a little later because I would love to explore that. And then they proceeded to talk about how much lesbian women and heterosexual women must begin to talk in order to understand what they have to learn from each other. I think maybe right now heterosexual women have a whole lot more to learn from lesbian women because there's an opening up there, an experience that we've all been silenced in. It does not mean that you have to define yourself, I don't think, as a lesbian woman to learn from that community and those women. But what the larger homophobic community puts upon us is that not only is it forbidden and something not to be explored, it also says you've either got to be one or the other and if you start being attracted to women sexually as well as emotionally or lovingly or whatever, then you're no longer heterosexual and you're probably lesbian. You're told that that's really bad, so you cut yourself off. That's one of the things I think is really powerful about what Dorothy said. How many of us have ever even explored the bisexual, the potential lesbian sides of ourselves without feeling like we have to give up what we know is still something that we are, the heterosexual side of ourselves? It's a question about that term bisexual that I think we've been really not allowed to look at.

LEE D.: I believe in speaking out and I do want to make a comment about the lesbian community. They have been the only people that have come out to answer any of my questions. I went through the most difficult time in my life in the past two years and any straight person—and I hate that word "straight" because that means everybody else is "bent"—but I would say that any heterosexual can't talk about it because they feel like, well, if you're not heterosexual then you're not important and plus we're women, we're supposed to love men, and so on. I owe a lot to a lot of the women I have met in this community. They have been the only ones that have said to me, it's your choice, go out and explore the world and whatever you decide is OK by us. I haven't heard that from anybody else and I don't expect I ever will. But that's something I want everybody to know, that we all have a freedom of choice in our sex lives, in our personal lives.

EVELYN FINGARSON: When I was at the Writer's Festival on Granville Island, a man by the name of David Young made a great point of saying that writers should work in the community. He said it's very important to get into all these other organizations, to start groups for this and that and to become known as a community person in order to further your ability and your success as a writer. It was my personal opinion that if you spend all this time in the community, you don't spend all that time writing. But I would like to get the reaction of the panel members on the extent to which you engage in community activity.

BARBARA HERRINGER: Well, I have worked for a number of years with social services and peripherally with groups in downtown eastside Vancouver as a result of that—outside of paid work. I also had an opportunity to work up north for a while with various community groups. I am now spending time with groups and individuals, and family and friends, who have AIDS. The writers that I know right now aren't just hiding out drinking scotch, smoking cigarettes and writing. First of all, nobody can afford scotch and cigarettes any more but also that is not how writers, or the men and women I know who are practicing their art, are living our lives. We can't, for one thing. We do need to work, and we tend to get involved in all sorts of activities in our community. I think it changes, and I think that, as Joy said, we move in and out of being political or taking active political part. My feeling is that when we go back and can spend some time in our homes, when we can actually distill where we've been working and write about it, that is a whole other political act. My feeling is that we are political beings regardless of who we are, but that's how we do work, that's where our writing comes from, that's where our words come from.

JOY KOGAWA: As to the question itself, when it presents itself to you, you know—am I going to write or am I going to this meeting? Which? That's the question I've been asking myself for the last five years practically every single day and I've been going to the meetings and I haven't been writing. I think a part of this panel was addressing the question, how do you sustain your spiritual legacy? I put my spiritual legacy ahead of everything else, I put it ahead of every other identity. And so the question for me was not, am I going to write? but, am I going to be obedient to my spiritual legacy? That is, how powerful is that spiritual legacy? I don't know how everybody else defines that for themselves. My sense from this group is that the call to liberation, the call to the freedom of your own beings inside of yourselves to be who you are, is a very powerful calling, and you're being obedient to it by bonding together and by strengthening yourselves, and if you're called to that you may not at that moment be called to your pen, you may be just called to that. I too was, I felt, while I was going to those meetings, being called to identify in the struggle against racism. It seemed to me to be a particularly virulent thing in this world and needed that effort on my part and there were lots of people who said to me, you know your greatest contribution to this whole struggle is to go to your pen and to write it out and to do it that way, and I would listen to that and I would believe that but there was something within me that wouldn't let me sleep at night. I had to get up and lick those envelopes, you know, and lick the stamps. There was nothing else I could do because I was so close to how much it hurt that there seemed to be nothing else except to be with the people, and if the time was going to come that I could write, I would wait for that time. My spiritual legacy has been one in which I fundamentally trust. I know that you can blindly trust, but there's a trust that's even beyond that, there's a deeper trust. I get that from my parents and I was obedient to that. So what I trusted was that if I'm supposed to write about it the time will come. Right now, I think I can write about it and I'm grateful for that, that I can actually make that choice. So I think each writer answers that question for themselves, at that point when they face it. If it doesn't hurt you so much that you can actually pick your pen up, in fact if picking your pen up and writing about it relieves you of that hurt, then I would say that's the thing to do.

LOUISE PROFEIT-LEBLANC: Well I'd like to try and respond to that. As I said, I'm not a writer, but I guess the pen does speak and in my own particular life I have opportunity to be with elderly people on almost a daily basis. Most of my time is spent listening and whatever opportunity I have, when an idea starts coming through, I just hope that I have a napkin or a pencil or a friend nearby that does have one and I just jot things down and thoughts come through—and if I'm close to a typewriter it's even better. But I've been beginning to network, and I was so happy to meet Viola and to get in touch with people who might even consider publishing some of these thoughts that for the most part, even in my own community, are so different. You know, sometimes I've given a couple of poetry readings and people have said, what are you talking about? and sometimes that's very difficult. Speaking to the spiritual legacy, this is what I have—that strong conviction that whatever I put down I would be able to understand a little more of myself, because in order to understand anything else you have to begin to understand yourself and to believe in that and to listen to what it says inside of you to do for that moment. I know one of the things that I'm beginning to learn, and that's from working with people who have been in violent relationships is—you know, we joke about it but we cry together and hug each other and I say, well, now you've lived through it, you have to write about it, because other people won't believe it until it's written. If it's not down on paper then it doesn't hold any substance. So we have to learn how to write and we have to learn how to express. I really loved what Lee said yesterday in the panel. She said, you know we have to learn how to articulate and we have to learn how to do it very well so that nobody can come back and say you really don't know what you're talking about. Because I think, for the most part, people do know what they're talking about, and if they have the opportunity to write it and fool around with it until it gets clear—it's like when you're stirring a sauce that has to come clear, you just keep stirring it and you know that it's going to come clear.

SKY LEE: I can say that I have worked very hard for my community. Now it's just a matter of defining that community. It's a little bit hard for me because I understand from feedback from my friend that I live in a world of my own, but maybe on the other hand that's what's saved me, because I can honestly say I have worked in many communities. I have worked in Chinatown—well, I was a young Chinese-Canadian searching for her identity. After that I went into the feminist community. I worked for *Makara* [magazine]. I saw that community through the eyes of a young Chinese-Canadian searching for her identity. Beyond that, I went into a community that everyone is very much a part of. I'm a nurse and I work with alcoholics and I work in what I call an alcoholic society and that's a much larger world. I have worked very hard and, as you say, every bit of it's contributed to my writing. Yes it's hard, you have to ream out the last of your energy to also write on top of that but ultimately that is, as I say, my way of striving for freedom and I don't resent having to do, you know, work to enhance my writing and I don't see the two as conflictive.

BARBARA HERRINGER: I wonder if I could just step back and maybe start to answer Sandy's question about heterosexual and lesbian women. I would like to start out with a small story. About twelve years or so ago, a man that I had been involved with for many years told me that he was gay. I was then in a relationship with another man and I got a letter from my friend who, now that I was safely with somebody else, could tell me that he was gay. Well all I wanted to do was sit down with him and ask him a million questions, like what was it like? how did he feel in his heart? I mean, how did he feel physically. When I first became a lesbian I also wanted the people that had been involved in my life to ask me what was going on for me right now, rather than me getting up everywhere I was and in the thrill of the moment basically telling everybody what was going on and then having them shuffle off. It became very uncomfortable, and I realized that this is not something that everyone else takes pleasure or joy in, that I better just cool it. I felt that a little bit this afternoon and I need to say this because I have been quite moved by this conference. I was extremely moved by Betsy and Louise's workshop this morning where we began to share some stories and I realized I couldn't speak—not because of who I felt I was, but because I felt like I didn't want to burst into tears in the workshop. That is how close to the surface I have felt. And going a little bit off track, when I began to speak earlier about what is important to us as lesbians, it's that we are able to speak about who we are sexually. I think that what has happened with a lot of lesbian writing as well is that there isn't a lot of talk about the erotic, there isn't a lot of talk about who we are as lovers or with one another, and I think that we need to be able to say that without people saying, we've heard enough. We haven't heard enough, we haven't even begun to tell enough about what has been going on in our lives. When I can say to a group of women here, well no, I don't think my sex life is the greatest at this point, what I want to be able to continue to say, without interruption, is that my partner and I also, as probably all of you, move through incredible cycles in our loving, and that we are, all of us as lesbians, moving on all sorts of planes here, and that to write or to speak about these things in front of others, even sometimes with our friends, gets very precarious. So I want to thank all the women who have been able to get up, and particularly one woman yesterday who was able to stand up and say for the first time in public, I am a lesbian. I'm very moved by all our lives here today.

PEG KLESNER: Well having done it once (*laughter*) . . . I just want to share, because it's on the same line as Barbara's, an experience. Two years ago I decided that it was time that my very close friends needed to know who I was. One friend was on a world trip and I decided that I would write to her and 'fess up. I had been reading all the latest literature from the lesbian community that said well now, when you tell your family (*laughter*) this is how you do it and it's very important that you allow them many opportunities to ask questions. So I said, when I meet you at the plane, if you want to ask me any questions please feel free. So about six months later I go out to the airport and I pick her up. We give each other a good hug and that's a good sign, I think, OK, I must be OK. And, total silence. I mean about the topic that I thought would come up. I had made up my mind before I went to the plane that if she wanted to talk about it, fine, but if she didn't want to talk about it I'd erase myself, as Lee put it so well yesterday. Eight months went by and finally the subject came up. She said to me, Peg, why do all of you feel you've got to tell us? And I was just flummoxed, I wasn't ready for the question at that moment. I guess I said to her: well, a) mental health (*laughter*) and, phew, that was pretty good, and then b) I said, in the hopes that when those of you who know us and love us realize that we're not "bent," that we are OK and that we're charming and interesting and as varied as possible, that it'll change the world a little bit. Because she comes from a minority group as well, she said, don't count on it. I've been fighting since 1966 and, as you well know, it's very hard to change attitudes towards my people. I looked at her and I said, but things have changed immensely since I was eighteen and admitted to myself that I was gay. And she said, how? I totally blanked out, I could not think of a single thing, I was just so tight and so worried about sharing. So, part of this pressure to share is so hard on us because we share a guilt that we don't deserve to have. We do need to have the heterosexual women who are our friends and our companions reach out to us, and I know it's hard for you but if you think it's hard for you, live inside our skins for a while.

UNIDENTIFIED SPEAKER: When I first realized I was a lesbian, one of the ways my identity really fell into place wasn't specifically sexually, it was through reading lesbian writers. I'd been reading poetry all my life and I could never figure out why my poetry didn't sound like Ginsberg and Layton, and as soon as I came out as a lesbian and started reading lesbian writers, I could figure out where my voice was and why indeed I didn't sound like the boys. I do want to pay tribute to Dorothy Livesay because ten years ago, before I realized I was a lesbian and I was drowning in a lot of misogynous male writers, there was a person who had a passion and seemed to have a love of being a woman and a very joyful, bright voice out of all this darkness, and that was Dorothy Livesay.

BETSY WARLAND [from the audience]: I have really appreciated how we keep coming back, spiralling around, to the importance of a sense of spiritual quest in our work and our living, which I often refer to as vision, and how that does weave us in and out of political action and sometimes very intense interpersonal reaction and sometimes very intense art-making, whether it's telling stories or writing them. So thank you.

Timmy Timms
photo: Evelyn Fingarson

Dorothy Livesay
photo: Evelyn Fingarson

Panel Two: Creative Writing

Joy Kogawa

(From a work-in-progress, tentatively titled **Itsuka.***)*

Sunday afternoon, September 1983.

I'm standing at the bus stop in the splattering rain, waiting for the northbound Bathurst bus, and here, unexpectedly out of the grimy air is a gift. It's as if I've been in a coma for years, in the debris at the side of the road, and suddenly—a presence by the roadside, tangible as an ambulance driver kneeling and doing mouth to mouth resuscitation and thumping a fist on my chest to get my heart moving and my lungs are filling. It's as if I can hear a voice calling my name through the blare and scuffle of traffic and I want to lift my arms up but I can only take a breath—a deep choking breath. But that's enough. Here. Waiting for the bus. Not moving at all. It's enough to be breathing.

"Thank you." The words come forth unannounced.

There's a promise in the air. I can touch it as surely as I touch the raindrops. I could throw my head back and laugh but the people standing by would say I've lost touch with reality.

Specifically, what I'm feeling is that it's all right. It's not what people say that matters. What's important is what precedes. It matters to stumble after. In the midst of all the unknown, it matters to trust. It matters in this time of not yet sight that some skin cells seem sensitized to light.

It might have been something like this in those murky days before there were eyes. Perhaps some of our jelly bodied cousins floating on the sea felt the sun beckoning forth feelers. And there they were, our primitive eyes, light sensitive cells in stamens of flesh quivering across the waters.

What frail creatures we are, yearning to know and desperate for what eludes us. We're a planet of snails with our not-yet eyes, our delicate horns, probing the windy currents of memory and meaning, seeking direction.

Here at the bus stop there's a whisper in the rain. There's a whisper of a promise in the siren's loud wail. Make way! Make way! Clear the roads in all directions. Clear the lungs, the throat. Clear out the pathways for breath to move through. There's a leaping within and a sure sense of promise. I can feel it precisely. Thank you for this.

Beneath my skin, a rainbow is forming and arcing its way past doubts and my so many, so present fears. How I do fear and fear. Let me count the ways.

I fear glances and sneers. I fear walking through the gauntlets of the judges in the world. I fear the mazes through which fear runs and the pathways of delusions that great fears create. And I fear the cunning of the body's inner foes. I fear touch as much as the inability to touch. So of course, I fear Father Cedric. But even more right now, I fear the loss of the rainbow that shines through the rain. I fear the loss. Cedric, Father Cedric, there are legions of fears.

I see Father Cedric as a deserter from the ranks of Fear's terrible army. Or a spy. A sort of clerical 007.

The first time I met him was seven years ago, 1976. That's the year Aunt Emily launched her new magazine *Bridge*. What a shock everything was that night in August when I arrived in Toronto. Even the weather. I wondered how the birds with their dry porous bones, could fly in the choking city air.

He was standing there, a rather slight and wiry dark haired man, extravagant with laughter and calling out "Hello!" He and Aunt Emily were waving wildly at the bottom of the airport arrivals escalator as I descended.

"Father Cedric, Chair of my Advisory Board, meet my one and only niece, Naomi."

Aunt Emily is so non-Japanese in her exuberance. She's a militant nisei, a second generation made-in-Canada woman of Japanese ancestry. She didn't stop talking from the moment she grabbed my shoulder bag until I fell asleep on the cot in her newly cleaned out study. Streams of consciousness are usually within but hers is a flood on public land.

"Couldn't get a flea in this room yesterday, Nomi," she said as we plopped my baggage onto an armchair. "Files up to the ceiling." She'd just finished moving her papers over to her new 'rabbit warren,' a spare back room in Father Cedric's chaplaincy office.

Bridge had started out years earlier as a small newsletter to her dispersed nisei friends. "The dispersed are the disappeared unless they're connected," she'd said. "If you aren't joined to those you love, your heart shrivels up and blows away in the dust. Whole countries get disappeared that way. It could happen to Canada." In 1976, *Bridge* was attempting to become a 'cross-cultural vehicle in a multicultural country.' She wanted a Japanese Canadian initiative to be a 'therapeutic voice reaching beyond itself without abandoning itself.'

My aunt has always been passionate in her commitment to Japanese Canadians and to Canada. "If we're to survive, we need to be in touch. We need communication—the CBC, the national railway, a national newspaper with real regional news, a good postal system. If our country isn't to erode away, our roots must be firmly interlocked," she says these days. She's not always successful in being heard, especially by separatists, but, "What's success?" she'll ask. "If you're doing what you have to do, that's success enough."

She still looked so 'young' back in 1976, her short streaked hair a thick mop of health. She was fifty-nine but could have been forty. I'd just made it to that age. No-one believed it. Neither did I. As for Father Cedric, he was ageless. He could have been thirty, or sixty, though I now know he's exactly my age. Two months older. I'd never seen such a jubilantly elfin smile. The laugh lines from his eyes ran down the sides of his face almost touching the laugh lines from his mouth going up. His embrace was as light and surprising as the touch of soap bubbles. I stumbled over my feet.

The problem is I can't be direct. My heart beats erratically when I have something to say. The other night with Father Cedric, I was stammering away like an adolescent. He held his head to the side and smiled. It was unnerving.

Nothing that ever happened back home in southern Alberta prepared me for Toronto and Father Cedric. This city is outer space, and Father Cedric, modern Anglican priest, college chaplain, is a Buck Rogers from another galaxy. At least in Granton and Cecil there were rules. But here? I didn't even know there was a Toronto rodeo when I was lassoed.

I used to feel so sorry for those roped and branded calves at the local rodeos, panting in the dust, their eyes bulging. But then there would be the moment of release. The rope would be cut and the legs kick free. It's almost like that, here at the bus stop. How long will it last—this uncanny sense of certainty that is already beginning to elude me.

Barbara Herringer

Jesus Only Loves Good Girls

She jerked awake and fumbled for the light beside the bed. Gran must have switched it off. She knew that one of these nights she would die in her sleep and if she did she would go straight to hell. She sat up and made sure not to lean against the wall so she would stay awake. But if she stayed awake she would start to think and would start remembering why she was afraid to die in her sleep and go straight to hell. She recited the twelve times table and the names of everyone who had ever sat in front or behind her in school. She hadn't minded being at her grandmother's other summers for part of the time but she felt different now. The days were too long and she was tired of trying not to remember she knew why her mother had left her here and taken her younger brothers back to the city. Her toe tangled around her rosary. Usually she kept the beads under her pillow in case she thought she should pray. But what was the use of praying these days if she had a mortal sin on her soul. She was worse than a murderer for sure, but even priests came into a condemned man's cell before he died. No one would walk into this room in the middle of the night to pray with her and forgive her. Serves you right, she could hear them say. Serves you right if you can't sleep for the rest of your life. Gran was snoring in the next room and she felt safe for a moment. What would Gran say, or Grandpa? She couldn't imagine Gran knowing what she knew. She heard Aunt Zoe get up to pee. Maybe I could crawl in with her she thought. No, she'd think I was a baby. She began singing, Oh boy when yurr with me, oh boy, the world to see that youuu belong to meeee . . . and fell uneasily to sleep. It was already so hot out she could see waves across the road. She was thinking again. She'd better run and join the other kids before she thought too much and threw up her breakfast like she'd done for the last three days. Sometimes if she concentrated really hard she could pretend that she was like her friends and lose herself in games. The kind where it was like you were somebody else and when Gran called you in for lunch you had to come back slowly to the grown-up world so you could hear what she was saying. That was harder these days. It was like there were two of her and one of her watched the other try to play and not think. Except that they both knew she really was thinking and that was the scary part. She came from the city. It was pretty small and there wasn't much to do but her friends were around. She wondered if this had ever happened to Lucy or Kathleen. Gran's town was really dinky and her house was right across from the school. Dad had gone right through grade twelve at this place but always liked to tell them how far he'd had to walk in the middle of a Saskatchewan winter and how every morning he had to run down to his dad's office to light the fire even before he'd had any porridge. Just as she left Gran's yard, Gran called her back to go and get a few things at Beezley's store. Get that look off your face Gran said. There were lots of Hutterites in town today. How could they stand wearing so many clothes. She wanted to hide herself in their long skirts and go off with them in a cart to their farm. Or go with that Indian girl who waved at her. Her brother wanted to be an Indian when he grew up so he could dance and live in a teepee like at the Stampede. Maybe she would go too and they could dance and forget everything. She wandered into the park beside the CN station. It was cool here and the sparse poplars swished a breeze across her face. Her mother had told her a story about the little girl who got lost at this station... Once upon a time a little girl's mother left her in Gran's yard for a moment while she ran into the house for her hat. When she came out a few minutes later the little girl was gone. The mother was so frightened that she ran up and down the streets of the small town asking everyone she met if they had seen a little girl about this high. Finally old Mrs. Foster said yes, she'd seen a little girl about that high with dark brown hair and big brown eyes trundling down Maple Street towards the train station. The little girl's mother ran as fast as she could and there, standing beside the westbound train looking ready to hop aboard, was the little girl. When she saw her mother, the little girl laughed and ran to greet her. Mother scooped her into her arms and carried her all the way to Gran's house and they lived happily ever after. Except the little girl didn't live happily ever after. She was at the same train station now wishing her mother would carry her home and tell her she could stop thinking. She had to hurry across to Beezley's now before Gran got worried and started calling around for her like she was a baby. She'd love to be a baby now. Sleepy and full of milk, close to her mother's breath, small enough to curl on her mother's soft stomach, mommy's hands stroking her skin. Her Gran's hands were rough and crooked except when she told stories. It was hard listening to the stories this summer. They were for children and she felt old. Even older than Gran. She wished she had never been born. Had never gone to a new school and met Mary. Then she could play and sleep and not have to try to stop thinking. She grabbed the groceries and remembered to thank Mrs. Beezley so she could say what a lovely, polite granddaughter Gran had. Beezley's store was almost the same as the one Mary took her to. Mary said the old man gives away candy—free. His store smelled of oil and licorice and cheese and sausage and maybe it didn't matter that he kissed her on the lips one day and said have some jujubes or a cigar. She took both and went back. Sometimes he put the closed sign on the door and told dirty jokes and rubbed himself between his legs. Once the real her disappeared and watched from the store ceiling when he touched her chest and congratulated her on the two tiny buds that he buffed with his papery white hands. Ugh. She ran through the heat clutching the groceries, passed the Blue Bird Cafe and Grandpa's office not stopping to wave or smile in case he could read her mind, and stumbled up Gran's verandah steps. Aunt Zoe had made her a cheese sandwich but she said she felt too hot and went to her room. One day the old man closed the store and took her into his stuffy brown office with a scratchy red blanket on the couch. His desk was thick with dust and papers and popsicle wrappers as though he was saving them to send away for a skull ring like the one she had turning green on her middle finger. He told her to sit on the couch as he fumbled with his zipper and pulled it down. Then he reached inside and pulled out a thin greyish thing and held it in his hand. Before she started to laugh her real self flew to the ceiling again and watched as his eyes got funny. He moved towards her other self and pulled down her underpants. She pretended she was playing statue and didn't blink when he brushed the grey thing between her legs and made small crackly sounds in his throat. Her real self bolted from the ceiling, grabbed her statue self and both of them scrambled for the locked door before he could wipe the spit from his lips. I'LL KILL YOU IF YOU TELL ANYONE, he screamed. She crashed into the old man's wife as she turned to race down the alley and didn't stop until she came to her secret place by the river where she threw up and cried until it got dark. Aghgh. This was the worst part of thinking. Remembering his face and the grey thing touching her. She tried to pray but knew it was hopeless because it was her fault. If only she could make her mind remember wonderful things like tobogganing down Deadman's Pass last winter or racing her bike down by the creek and beating Lucy by a mile or the day she made the perfect shoestring tackle on Danny. That was the day before Sister Gabriel told her to stay after school because someone wanted to see her. As soon as she saw the lady walk into the classroom she knew she'd been caught. The grown-ups knew about the old man and would put her in jail. Did he tell on her? She was scared but she slouched in her desk like a hood so the lady wouldn't notice. The lady said she was a social worker and that someone had called her about the old man. The next afternoon she sat on her mother's bed while her mother told her the facts of life from a small pink book with stick drawings. Her mother wanted to know if the old man had touched her, what he had done to her. She tried to blurt it out but then it was like her mother didn't know what to say so they both sat there with words ready to burst off their tongues and she could hear her brothers out on the street and longed to be a boy and not this stupid girl who always got caught and was sure to go to hell and burn forever because of what she'd made the old man do to her for candy. There was Jesus on the crucifix above her parents' bed and somehow she really didn't believe that he died for her sins like the nuns said. Who ever heard of a sin like this and besides, the Blessed Virgin wouldn't have let the old man within a foot of her. Finally her mother got up and tucked the pink book in her dresser drawer and they went downstairs. Her father was reading the paper and mother said well, she's all ready for life now. Her father only stared at her and went back to his paper without a smile or a hug which is what she wanted and she ran outside and wondered how she could get out of this town. Gran was calling now so she rolled off the bed and decided to pretend she was just a girl visiting her grandparents. Grandpa would be home for supper soon and maybe later when it wasn't so hot she'd try going outside again. Maybe tonight she'd be able to sleep. After all, the old man's store was closed down a few weeks ago. But she could still see his face and he might track her down. No, he was too old and he'd never find her here, so far from everything. Maybe she'd just stay in tonight and ask Gran for a story and sit here with the grown-ups for awhile. They might even ask her to do her Ed Sullivan imitation again and tell her how clever she is with voices. Then her aunt would sit back in the old chair and say oh, to be a young girl again with nothing to worry about during these long summer days.

Sounds I make

for Stephen
(1949—1989)

sounds i make
the sOUNds i make the
SOUNds i make after i've held you
bird bones in my hand the shoulders
of you like bird bones the childsbody
mansbody tiny bones wrapped in wool
against my breast the sounds my heart
makes as you tell stories our story when
you used to hold me in your mansbody and
the sounds i made the
sounds you made our bodies making
sOUUNds

late afternoon sun dapples your
face as you lie in the nest of my bed
gathering your bird bones closer against
a chill
and i bring tea and you begin another story
unravelling tales like colored webs unfolding
and i crawl in beside you abandon the tea
burrow alongside your shrunken body
and gather you in my arms and my breath (sucks in)
remembering your shoulders your thighs
and torso remembering the strength of you
when we were lovers
a life
time ago

Oh
the SOUNDS i make after
i've held you

Sky Lee

from "Nancy Drew Mysteries"

Nancy bargained her way back to safe and warm. If she is very frugal, she tells herself, then she and her baby can stay holed up for a long time, until Gregg forgets about her. What is she anyway but a petty thief hiding out with mankind's most prized possession—the ownership of women's bodies.

But Gregg can't possibly know that she is carrying this baby. Even if he does hire some thug to come after her and his money, she can make herself into one of those invisible, dark-skinned streetgirls with the soddened bellies and chewed up faces. She is good at disguises.

But if he finds you, you're dead meat! You know that. Fuck! Why do you fucking think like that? Leave us alone! We're all safe. You know that! You've been watching, sensing. There's nobody out there. Get up, and look! Fuckin' look! Then shut up, and leave us alone!

She shouldn't have gone out. That was it. Stupid. Now, look what has happened! The baby has come loose. And she is afraid.

Nope, the baby is safe. There has been spotting all along. As long as it stopped, everything was all right. She could phone the hospital, but they'd only make her come in, and lay around, senselessly. They already have a thick file on her. She didn't want to go in, having already exhausted what little energies she's had for people tonight!

Nancy went back to playing with her baby in her stomach. She liked the idea of being a mummy, and giving mother-scented kisses. She had wonderful ways of finding and tickling its precious little butt—when it poked out, she poked in. Oh look! Memories. Look and see! See Nancy! See Nancy when she was very, very little.

◇

On that old, scratchy, fold-down couch, of long ago, beside a little electric heater, which gave off precious little heat, she woke up. The air was cold and damp, but she was warm enough under the blankets, and there was nowhere else in the world she would rather be, except snuggled tight as she could against her mum. She got up to look around.

"Nancy, are you cold, baby girl?"

"No, Mummy, I'm not. Mummy, are you still waiting for Daddy?"

No answer. She wanted to look out the window. Maybe Daddy was out there on the street. If she saw a man walking by, she thought it was her daddy. She didn't run to tell Mummy though. She watched him walk quickly, until it was too dark to see him.

"Nancy, don't squirm so much. You might wake Bobby."

"Mummy, I'm cold," whined her little brother.

"Squeeze in against me tightly, Bobby. Nancy, lay down."

Nancy lay down. She wanted to feel her mother's warm breath on the top of her head.

Then she got bigger—big enough for raging. She saw him pin her mother down like an animal. Her mother was too weak and bruised to resist him. Her dress torn, her spirit hunted down, she lay limp and still under him. Nancy and Bobby had been hiding in the dark corners of the house, but the drunken yells, and the crashing about got worse. Then the silence. Most terrifying, she needed to see what was that silence. She crept out with Bobby close behind her. She saw. Him pulling out his dink, like he was going to piss on her mother. Red fury whipped around her; she shrieked at him. Pounced on him with all her being. He toppled easily. Bobby pulling at his mother to get away. Her mother came back to life, pulling at Nancy to get away. Nancy stood entranced, at the door, and watched her father shit-faced, struggling to his knees, his thing hanging out of his pants. He bent forward, and started to pee. Nancy tried to let go, but no matter how hard she tried, she couldn't be pulled away from the endless splatter of his urine on the carpet.

The tainted smell of home kept her away, but she learned to get along real well on the outside. She learned how to ask for things. And where to get them. She learned to pick and choose from among the giveaways. Which ones had strings attached; which ones didn't. All these things she learned early. Because the ghosts of women taught her well. Protect yourself. Protect your sex. Protect your heart.

Gregg liked, wanted, required her to keep fresh-cut flowers all over his house on a hillside. It had a "melon dalla" view of the city, sprawled out, spilled, spread eagled under its own toxic cloud. Sunlight swarmed through the patio glass; the huge bouquets in their elegant vases exploded in fits of passion, raining pastel shimmer off the cathedral-like ceiling. The air intense, and fragrant; Nancy wore sunglasses to read.

Gregg asked her if she wanted a flower garden. He told her to hire a landscaper, to put in whatever she wanted. But no, she only wanted cut flowers to primp, to play with. She found out about the early morning markets before dawn, and along with the chinese green grocers, went to choose buckets of the freshest blooms. Like everyone else, she bought a styrofoam cup of steaming coffee for a quarter, and haggled over price. "Where you' store, ledy," they asked her. For a few moments, she thought she really was what she pretended to be. Somebody who belonged to somewhere.

The memory of the feel of a woman's belly carried Nancy a long ways. Three years, she stayed with Gregg, because she didn't want to be like that? Who wants to be like that? Three years, she read what she wanted to read; she studied what she wanted to study; she drove to art classes in any one of his cars. It wasn't real, it wasn't going to last. She knew that; Bobby knew too!

"Bobby! Bobby, where the hell are you? Wacha' doin' there? How much? How the hell am I going to get that much?"

Gregg was too busy, being the hot-shot white boy to understand. He had much too much of everything. Being unethical, of course, he still wanted more. Maybe she played the part of his slit-slut too well, purring on cue, as he nuzzled her constantly, his hands hard on her butt, suggestively brushing her nipples as he talked business buddies.

He was too fucking privileged to understand anything else. Gregg thought he was making business deals for fun and games. Him plenty big man, plenty big heart, plenty big smarts. He secure in his cliques; she stripped bare and flayed open by their women.

Nancy used to stare down their hatred like a rockface about to landslide, but it didn't make for nice, candle-lit chitchat at the dinner table. So, in order to please their men, the women learned to ignore each other, sneering behind the phoney smiles.

Nancy wondered why she was so alien to these women, until she discovered that where she was playing for fun, they were playing for keeps. Aah, well then, where she could see the game through to the end, they would impale themselves on the revolving spokes. She would stay with the role of whore, but they wanted to be wife. In their dress, they tried to disguise their motives in wishy washy colours, in confusing tiers of ruffles, and flimsy lace. In their souls, they were already wrung-out, prepared for mediocrity. Brazenly sexual, Nancy dressed for shock and drama. She aimed for purity and lawlessness.

Nancy heard about one couple heading home in their cars, the woman's venom unleashed. "Bitch! What is there to say to a slant-eyed whore like that. Makes me want to puke. It's degrading enough that you make me sit at the same table as her."

They made their men sheepishly conform, but only for the moment. In men's eyes, Gregg may be a chink-lover, but in their cut-throat business, he can only be kicked in the head when he's down. While he's on top, it was the better part of valour to find someone else to boot. The woman was dispensable at best, particularly if she couldn't find a way to pay obeisance to the not-so-complicated order of the good ol' boys.

Really, they were all thieves and murderers. They had no conscience. Why did that jerk tell her that story anyways? Never fight evil, thought Nancy, it will eventually eat itself up.

Gregg never knew about her brother's death. He never wanted to know her family, and she never offered. Bobby was the only one anyways, and Bobby couldn't keep up with her. For the life of him, he couldn't do it.

"Run, Bobby, run!"

"I can't. I can't."

"HURRY! COME ON!"

So he had to go and get himself killed. Maybe he killed himself. Fuck you, Bobby. Fuck you all to hell. Can you imagine? Burnt to a crisp on some flea-bitten mattress up north somewhere.

And then, she had to go and get pregnant. She could have had an abortion; if he knew, Gregg would have made sure she was vacuumed out. See, honey, here today, gone to Maui! One thing in common with those other broads, she didn't last in the end either.

◇

A feverish wanting to scream deep in her throat woke her up. She retched into consciousness. She had fallen asleep? She must have. She had had a dream, the sensation of it horrible. She dreamt that her saliva had an infestation of fleas. Every time she opened her mouth, and gave them oxygen, they came to life, and sprang out of her mouth by the hundreds, wet and squirmy, onto her quilt. She feels like vomiting, the tension around her head makes her panic. "You're safe. You're safe," she is panting, wet with perspiration. Still, waves of shame wash over her. Still, she can't cry yet.

Bobby was nineteen. "Bobby, call me!"

Nancy hadn't heard from him in a couple of months, and that worried her because, no matter how bad, how poor, how sad, they usually kept in touch every week, every two weeks, a month at most. She used to think that he was a pain in the neck, always in trouble, always borrowing money. He never listened to her.

"Got a twenty you can lend me, Nancy?"

She finally phoned the RCMP. They asked her about his teeth. Were they all rotten? She imagined charred remains with rotted teeth hanging in there. She remembered how he used to wake her up in the middle of the night, desperate for help. His teeth rotted out even before they grew in. She fed him adult strength aspirins, crushed them up and stuffed them into his gaping cavities. Yes, she answered, he has very bad teeth. Her voice clinked like ice; she refused to cry. Why cry over nothing. How did she know that he ever existed at all. Like Nancy didn't exist either, really.

She felt another spasm. She looked at the clock. Two thirty-eight. Scary. She knew she had to go to the hospital this time for sure. Suddenly, she thought of something which she had missed. A missed detail in her meticulous getaway plan. Suddenly, she knew how Gregg would find her. The hospital. So very obvious too. Any hired thug with a phone. "Patient information. Ward Two south, sir. You're very welcome, sir."

She's going to be in a shadowy hospital room, see, with operating lights glaring down on her throbbing pain. All around the room, there will be wrapped bodies, masked faces, gloved hands, eyes of newt. Then, she'll smell him, his cologne, his Gitanes, his newly starched clothes. He will suddenly be there in the room with her, stomping on her attempts at rebirth. He will remind her that in order to be reborn, she still has to face her endless emptiness. She will read his terrible thoughts.

"I'm going to get you, Nancy, I'm going to fix it so you never get away from me again."

He would pay her back for withholding from him; he would destroy her if she did not submit. "How much you embezzle off me, Nancy?"

"You gave me that money. I didn't steal it."

"I bought you clothes, jewelry, pleasure, toys, trinkets, knick-knacks. What, am I stupid enough to pay you to dump me?"

"No, Gregg, bad for the ego!"

"Fucking rights, honey!"

Not freedom, never freedom, Nancy. Go straight to jail! Nancy lay there in the dark. Listening. She tensed when she heard it, because when she heard it, she recognized it right away. Don't you see what fear is. Listen. Outside, below her window, along the sidewalk, the sound of a woman's high-heeled shoe scraping the pavement. Slow, the drunken, drugged staggering under the anger; the footsteps of hopelessness. In fuck-me shoes. Aimless, stumbling. Two forty A.M. A hacking cough. The air cold and wet. Tonight, the night restless.

Louise Profeit-LeBlanc

Sister Greyling

Caches emptied, only leg bones left.
Where the caribou once roamed
There was nothing now!
Even the rabbits vanished.
The time of starvation was here . . .

The man looked at his wife, so weathered and thin.
Breasts emptied of their milk
A babe's crying ceasing to faint whimper,
Weak in his mother's arms.
Sunken eyes and fontanelles.

He sharpened the knife.
The job would have to be done quickly
As the cold would take you down.
Making you like itself.
Where was the fatty flesh?

Out onto the stark white lake,
Glowing in the dark,
All was quiet in the morning
Except for the interaction
Of the snowshoe against the snow
And his breathing.

He had kept the hole open for water
And pulling the tarp off,
Looked into the murky, black waters
Steaming below in the moon-lit morn.
Murmured softly to his Maker.

Swift as the movement of his knife
On an animal's body, he braced himself
And face grimacing with pain
Cut off a small piece of his own flesh
Wrapped it quickly with moss and skin.

Letting his breath out again
Placed the life giving flesh
On the hook and lowering it into the water,
He waited.

The greyling came . . .
And starvation left.

1987

The Old Man and the Swans

After their journey northward
The swans had finally made their way
To his bay.

Out on the beach
On his faithful old bench, with his
Ol' fashioned "field glasses"
The old man gazed out onto the ice.
Not hearing, only seeing . . . enjoying.

The sun so intense
That at first it was impossible to see
Those magnificent birds, white on white
The camouflaging effect. Such a delight!

His heart was racing
As he scanned the horizon.
And then . . . Yes! There they were full of life
Swooping gracefully down onto the ice.
Porcelain grace, feminine in stature
Necks curling backwards, tucked under
Their wings.

"They must be tired!" the old man thought.
They've had such a long trip.
The glasses now focused on a swan's head
Beginning to dip
Into the icy waters.

"My old friends, welcome back!
Thank you for bringing back spring and
Informing the lake of the impending summer."

Up into the air
They all begin to rise
At the precise moment of his thought.

Winging a circle around their chosen spot.
Gradual movements up and down
Of their wing span.
Black beaks, eyes, feathers so smooth
And stark.
In unity. In perfect form. A decision
Was now made for them to embark.

Marshlake swans silhouette the black spruce
Glowing on the snow.
The same encore from so long ago.
A comfort and a pleasure
For the old man.

"There he is! The old man!
It's his longing and wish that
Brings us here
To the part of the lake
That he holds so dear.

How hunched over his old shoulders seem.
Has he had a long winter, a death?
Or is it just his age that now has deemed
That illness, loss of hearing, family
Problems become part of the test?
Thank God he has his wife to care.

Yes it is your beckoning wish that is
Our command
To fly here to your bay to land
And bring you all the joy
That old age demands!"

1985

PART TWO

Voice(s)-Over

Lee Maracle

Ramparts Hanging in the Air

I warn myself before I leave my insulated world and attempt to connect with white Canadians at the TELLING IT conference that in a racially dichotomized society in which white supremacy colours everyone's attitude this connection is bound to grate against the flesh. There are moments when this expected discord does not occur; unfortunately such moments are rare. On the bright side, we are telling it exactly the way we see it, feel it, experience it and there is an audience engaged in the business of really listening, trying to feel and experience our lives in an honest fashion. Hope is no longer a phantom which haunts those without future, but is a promise to tomorrow that things will be different for women of colour.

One of the advantages of being the speaker is having the first word; the advantage of being one of the editors has also given me the last word. My last words are oriented to those women who write, and whom I identify as intellectuals striving to cut through the lies of their lives to assemble some of the wonderful truths of their humanity. TELLING IT was difficult. Difficult, because the women came from so many different cultures. We gathered in a building in the downtown core of what is now known as Vancouver, not far from Vancouver's version of Wall Street. I was born not far from here at a time when the Vancouver Hotel was the tallest building—now the European Big Houses stretch skyward in their multitudes and dwarf the old Hotel, creating a claustrophobic cluster not far from my place of birth. I think about how curious it is that not a single soul has ever asked me what this place was known as before they came. I realize that culturally Europeans do not feel the same about birthplace as I do—they would not call themselves Canadians if they did. But still the lack of curiosity about me runs deeper than just birth place; it governs a lot of social and personal interaction, mostly failed interaction, between myself and Europeans. Some women are wont to use the term "threatened" by "them/the other." One only feels threatened by outsiders if one doubts their insides. Failed cultural interaction between myself and European women cannot be dismissed as simple "threat of other" psychology. There is a tendency among Europeans to treat human relations in the same fashion as they do money relations: debit, credit, balance and reconciliation; you do this for me and I expect you to do that for me and if you don't, everyone else will hear about it. Great expectations. The reality is that almost nothing we see and experience in this world has the same value: relatives, life, death, friendship, support, loyalty, all hold different weight and manifest themselves differently. We all keep repeating ourselves as though the general theories had no practical manifestation. We accept in theory that we are culturally separate, yet, in practice, we lash out if the actual interaction is not up to our expectations. I know all this and I think about it before I reach the platform. How am I going to say this again and be heard and understood?

Every woman came full of her own presence. They did not come meek and full of awe for the speaker's platform, for which I am exceedingly grateful in hindsight only. They brought with them ideological and political persuasions, emotions and thoughts and they put them on the table for the speakers to examine. Challenge permeated the atmosphere. They also brought with them whatever remnants they had of the patriarchal and racist culture from which we were all nurtured. That was difficult. It had been twenty years, almost to the day, since I had begun my own personal struggle against racist and patriarchal dogma. This forum numbered in the three hundred plus times that I had spoken on essentially the same subject. I take it on. I have never been short of courage. My mind looks about me at the women. I decide what I am going to say and find a corner to write it out.

I was sitting at the table, high above all the people as we are still wont to do at such events, just feeling the tension coming from some of the women. It was thick in the air, tangible, and it rent great holes in me. Jeannette felt it too. We held hands for a moment, rooting ourselves in our own places and dug deep inside ourselves for the words, special words, that would finally begin to build the ramparts to the bridge which would allow us to meet as equals. Those ramparts are still hanging in the air in that room, dusty and unused.

"So What if You're a Different Colour?"

Dorothy Livesay, a feminist treasure, an elder, a poet, a social activist and a woman with a huge heart and a great passion for truth speaks. She refers to herself as a WASP. Paragraphs of complaint come from several women accusing the speakers of uttering the ultimate insult. During the confusion Dorothy attempts to take responsibility for her words, but no one hears, not even the machine taping the words. I read my defence with some embarrassment now. In a racist society the cultural interaction of citizens is bound to be racist. Racism in this country means white supremacy. Our response to this phenomenon is survivalist, not racist. We know we are going to be carved up and no one is going to object. None did. I have had this experience before; frankly it is a tired old re-run from a sorry ass set of relations that ought to have Canadians thoroughly embarrassed by now. We are invited to speak and everyone sits waiting in ambush, waiting for us to slip up, indicate some form of discriminatory behaviour so they can justify not listening to anything else we say. That is what happened.

The scariest part is they did not listen to each other. Given the structure of internal disrespect, be it internal racism or internal sexism, the subject of discussion ceases to exist without respect for the speaker. What frightens me now is not so much that our denial was not believed, but some of the women did not listen to their own elders. Cultural difference abounded in the moments of exchange after our presentations. First, no Indigenous person has ever been credited for this but we are scrupulous about *not* publicly accusing someone of saying something they did not say. We verify what we think they said first. Second, we accept their version of what they said for two reasons: one, the person must retain their dignity, and challenging their credibility is humiliating, and second, having asked the question the speaker may have re-thought out what they said and changed their minds, which we believe they are entitled to do in the smoothest and most dignifying way possible. And lastly, we listen when elders speak. Dorothy Livesay is not just an old woman, she is a golden treasure that the feminist movement is as yet unable to appreciate.

It didn't end there. In one of the workshops a woman said, "[. . .] I learned a lot from the panel last night [PANEL ONE: Jeannette, Betsy, Lee], and I think that's where I learned a lot about labelling [sic]. I mean, we're different colours, but we're equal. And I saw other women didn't think we were equal, you know, everyone somehow wanted to have a label. And I wanted to go and speak and say, 'Hey wait a minute. We're all women, we're all equal, so what if you're a different colour?' [. . .]" Very patriarchal and very racist. Simply repeat the tired old story of white men, substituting colour for woman in the appropriate spaces: "So what if you're a woman, we're all equal, we're all people, etc." There has been no revolution in this country in my lifetime. Given that inequality was structured into every institution in this country from its inception, it is safe to assume just the opposite; inequality still dogs people of colour. It can never be eradicated by people who say "so what?"

My mothers did not enjoy the privilege of being born *Canadian*. They did not enjoy the privilege of access to libraries, a liberal education, or any of the amenities of being born Canadian. They still do not enjoy life in this country. No great novels of the struggle of humankind for justice, liberation and equality dotted the landscape of their academic life; only the robes of the church, the songs of Gregorian priests and the great common kitchens and agricultural fields of industrial residential schools existed for them, but then we said that and the woman who said "so what" did not hear. No quiet winter nights with mothers and grandmothers speaking in soft voices, telling endless stories to teach them how to be; only the solitude of dormitories in which children from different nations, speaking different languages lengthened the loneliness of their childhood. None of the wonderful verses of Dorothy Livesay, Pat Lowther or Pauline Johnson in which they may have been able to envision themselves marching towards freedom and a future existed for them.

No local school-boards or political organizations to which to take their complaints, no vote to alter the politics of their reality existed for them. I have heard white women utter in speeches that universal suffrage, women's suffrage is some sixty years old. That is not our reality and do we not count as women in this country? No, we are not equal. We live half as long, are unemployed, impoverished as a people. No youth should ever have to attend the funerals of thirty-seven young relatives and friends, grow up to watch her children weep with hunger, search for work and be told "the position is filled" by employers who continue to advertise, or be told that she is "not qualified to be trained," as I and now my children and the majority of Native women are told over and over again. Half of the women in our community are single, near-destitute mothers. Half of the children apprehended each year by the Ministry of Human Resources are our children. No, we are not equal and I don't believe the woman who said that is blind. I believe she is uncaring.

No one from the panel to which she referred was at the workshop in which she made the remark. Hence, we could not take exception to it. She "wanted to say," but she didn't. In our segregated worlds lie truth and fiction, fear and courage. The lie in your life is that it doesn't matter. If it didn't matter you would have said it to us, not about us, and attempted to convince us of the veracity of your remark. The truth of our lives is that it does matter; the lies and truths we labour under silence us. Your refusal to speak to us then silenced us.

When a white woman says, "So what if you are a woman of colour," she does not want to hear my story, she does not want to tie the thread of her history to mine, she wishes to bury my history in the clothes of her own. The world is not a flat white world in which I lie buried underneath. Should this country succeed in breaking the thread of my history, the fabric created will be bland, lacking in colour, wanting difference.

The truth of my life and my mother's life belongs to you; you created it with your acceptance of our death and destruction, but you do not own me. "We are all women... " You cannot lay claim to me outside of my truth. I refuse to uproot the silken, delicate and beautiful thread of thousands of years of my history and ride piggyback on the short thread of yours. We both ascend this mountain of lies inherited by a racist and sexist society from different sides; should I scurry to your side, ride on your back to the summit, I shall arrive without knowledge of my own. We shall both reach the summit, half-ignorant, half-knowing, half-understanding the world and the ascent to truth. I am not half-assed about anything.

"Is Lesbian a Culture?"

I wish the remark had come from a white woman. It would have been easier to dismiss it as homophobic, sexist nonsense. I wish it had come in the context of a great rallying to our defence against those women who wrongfully accused us of calling them "names, labelling them WASPS, hurting them," etc., but it didn't. It came from a woman of colour amid the silent belief by the women we were addressing that we were naughty little coloured girls who had called them WASPS. Amid the paragraphs of bogus accusations hurled at us, I had begun to feel trapped, on the run to a very small corner. I wanted to drift off into apathetic silence and just wait out the evening. The remark woke me up.

A piece of me respects her, she at least said it to the organizers who were there, unlike my "so what" friend. Answering it was not easy at the time. I knew it would cost me a newly-won friend, a woman of colour I had just begun to know. A friend who would not be found in the obit column too soon. My dad reminded me the other day of something our grandmother had told us: "Don't be fooled by these people. Given a choice between friendship and their anti-racist principles, they will take the word of their friend and you will always have to prove yourself. We aren't like that . . . " So here I go publicly dissociating myself from homophobia in the absence of white lesbian feminist dissociation from false accusations of some very defensive racists. We are not equal even when we rebel.

I don't know why I continue to quickly calculate the cost of doing the right thing—the price I inevitably and consciously pay has never deterred me—but I suppose the influence of capitalist-accounts-receivable-culture is strong in my mind, because I always tally up and then do the right thing anyway. I lost a possible friend. That doesn't seem like much, but given the reality that once every couple of months some Native friend or relative dies on me, those of my friends whom I know will survive take on near-sacred significance, not to be let go lightly. But I know, if I remain silent I will erase myself—not something I cherish.

Everyone has a perfect right to be. Lesbian women, of which many are women of colour, have suffered a specific kind of erasure that can be articulated only by conscious Lesbian writers striving to give voice to their specific struggle to be.

Since writing is a cultural endeavour, Lesbians must enjoy their own cultural specificity. That is logic. My logic is simple, uncharged by the derisive laughter of my community on whom I depend for my livelihood and free of the tired old nineteenth century notion that "culture is based on language." Indigenous people do not cloak their raw emotions, no matter how reactionary, in rational clothes. "This is very painful to me"—and we were given the question, alongside the answer and the derision of her community. I know a little something about technique: when a speaker asks a question and answers it, the question is rendered rhetorical, not requiring an answer. Still we answered.

That was a year-and-a-half ago. The question, rhetorical as it was, was never answered. The speaker defined culture as "based on language." This is a tired old definition that has some serious problems. First, for a thing to exist, concept or otherwise, it must truly be separate and enjoy a definition that separates it from other things. "Culture is based on language"—although we have serious misgivings about the truth of this, we always seem to find ourselves defending our right to be, rather than trashing this definition. Let us supply it with a small dose of backtracking Indigenous logic. There we are, a half dozen or so of us people sitting around a fire some 150,000 years ago. We have been sitting doing nothing for days, maybe weeks, who knows, but we are not interacting because of course, language, not culture came first. Finally to everyone's great relief some genius—likely a 'male hunter' if anthropologists be believed—decides to do something with the rest of us bumps on our hill. To communicate his desire to do he must conjure a word or two in order to describe it: lo and behold language! After that some other little genius discovered that language can be put to use not just for the practical purpose of working together, communicating together for our common survival, but we can use it to sing! Oh, happy day! Now we have both language and culture. I am sorry, but I cannot believe that interaction did not precede language. Interaction between people, the establishment of relations either organically or consciously, is what culture is all about. Language is one means of expression of culture, but it is not the main expression. We allow science to "culture" bacteria, but for humans to be culturally distinct they must have a distinct language. "Englishness" is a whole set of mores, codes, defined interactions, assumptions and relationships replete with power relations. Black North Americans, Mexican North Americans, Native North Americans, Asian North Americans and White North Americans speak English—many as their *only* language. We are not the same culturally. The practice of whining is acceptable in white society, not so in mine. It forms an important component in Black humour, not so in white society—although this is changing among women somewhat. Indigenous people enjoy hours of amusement recalling all the complaints they have ever heard, usually uttered by white folks, laughing until their sides ache.

Interaction around eating, working, living, rights to privacy, respect for space territory—all are cultural. Songs, stories, dance, language all reflect and articulate culture, but language is not the basis for it any more than song or dance. As a young person I asked both my European instructor and my Native instructor the same question; the answer was radically different. The one a lecture, essay-style response, the other a story, a riddle I would have to figure out. Same language, same question, different interaction.

Cultural difference is conditioned by two things: internal distinctiveness, and external conditions, the latter being the weaker of the two. There is a huge difference between Lesbian women and women who are not lesbians. The interaction between is different. A good many of us are smug about being able to identify that this woman is gay as though the difference were a superficial empirical difference. Just like my "so what" friend who put the difference between myself and her as a simple matter of a crayon. When someone denies the preponderance of culture among Lesbian writers then they labour under the misconception that the nature of the interaction between Lesbian women *as a community* is the same as it is for those outside that community, or they don't want to know what the difference is. I confess, culturally I don't want to know this either, but then I don't want to know the specifics of anyone's lust/love homo- or hetero-sexual, and therein lies all our sickness. Homophobes, dyed in the wool, and those struggling with it, all seem to reduce Lesbian culture to sexuality. We leave out the spirit of community that has been cultivated between these women this society has been trying to erase for 2,000 years. Cultural interaction is social and not primarily individual.

Well, if I don't want to know, then why do I read Lesbian literature and struggle to understand their sense of community, sexuality, spirit? Because I need to. I need to know. Whether or not this new knowledge is going to grate against my flesh culturally seems irrelevant to me. Homophobic silencing of Lesbian women will impede my quest for knowledge only for a moment. Repression will lead to resistance and although I do not understand Lesbian culture I do know about resistance. Silence is no longer a weapon of resistance for us, it has become our main means of implosion—turning in on ourselves.

Oddly enough, white as the woman who said she didn't care about women of colour was, and coloured as the woman of colour who denied voice for Lesbian women was, both shared something in common—denial of a people's right to be. In the end, it is for my self that I oppose silencing of Lesbian women, not because I seek allies among them, but rather that I choose to preserve myself: my sense of humanity is violated if another human being is offended. I want to tell my dad that I understand something about what t'a'ah was saying. We are not dichotomized, our thinking and our being are one and the same, a violation of our thought is a violation of our being. A friend who violates our thought also violates our being. It has nothing to do with lofty principles of support for one's fellow human being. I always felt uncomfortable speaking up because someone might think I was supporting them; in fact, I believe we all ought to be self-reliant and when someone speaks out against racism they are not supporting me, but rather defending their own perfect right to be. When they don't oppose racism, sexism and homophobia, they are likewise exercising a different right to be—they are not deserting anyone but themselves if their silence arises out of fear and not racist, sexist or homophobic conviction.

TELLING IT was difficult because we are still telling it, not moving with it. I dream of the day when remarks such as "so what if you're a woman of colour?" and "is Lesbian a culture?" will stop all the proceedings, and everyone will say, "Let's thrash this out, let's settle it, let's keep going until we come to a common agreement—consensus—because we aren't going anywhere if we don't." We all struggled to build bridges at the TELLING IT conference. Too bad they weren't located in the same spot directly across from each other.

I am back in my own world about to enjoy a cup of tea around the soft brown colors of my oak table in the quiet of my kitchen. My daughter walks in and gets on the phone.

"Hello, Tim Horton's Donuts? I am inquiring about your advertisement for a job. Yes. Is it still available? It is. Well asshole, why did you tell me it was filled!" She hangs up and starts looking up the Human Rights Commission number. I did not fix the world for her like I promised twenty years ago, but I did change something. Silence. Passive resistance is no longer our way of being. I watch her. Like me she is fighting back. Unlike me the fight seems to energize her, give her life. For her, hope is not a promise to tomorrow that things will be different; she has already decided she has a right to any future of her own choosing and if the world will not give it to her she is going to fight until she gets it. If I had not opposed the erasure of Lesbian women, of women of colour, she would not be fighting back—we would both be crying. Change is about being different; it is not about supporting this or that struggle, it is about being different. It is personal, in the sense that you take charge of yourself, own your convictions or lack of them and pursue them. Change is about never allowing someone to be silenced while you are there to speak. Change is not tolerating injustice. It is not about friendship, or supporting individuals because they are your friends. It is about personally taking on a different view of the world. No one supports me because I need it, but because they are against the racial inequities built into this system, and those inequities violate white people and coloured alike. Institutional inequity and passive acceptance of inequity by white Canadians prohibits your accessing me in any way, shape or form. Inequity denies you access to our different knowledge and experience; it condemns white folks to being half-smart, half-human.

Lee Maracle: Afterword

Canadian white women have made some great changes, but together we have a great distance to travel. We have taken the first steps towards a new humanity. We look a little odd—most of us are well over thirty and ought not to be still toddling and faltering—but through the organization of such gatherings as the TELLING IT symposium, we are on our feet and on our way. Panic sets in: here we are toddling when we need to race. Time, the old infidel, threatens us all. The engineering students of the University of British Columbia have again insulted the humanity of this country with their recent racist, sexist publication and we have yet to resolve enough of the conflicts between us to immediately put an end to such publications. The entire country has moved to the right. Racist violence, family violence, etc., is on the upcrease. Abortion is no longer clearly a choice we as women have. We have no time to lose and yet we are fractured. We as writers, keepers of the truth, must struggle modestly and quickly to come together. We cannot afford to be isolated and yet we still insulate ourselves against those with whom we have differences. We freeze at every suspected infringement on our perfect right to be. We are paralyzed by what may be construed as racism, sexism or homophobia in our ranks.

We need to "chill out," to use a contemporary expression. We must come to really feel that differences are not personal: they come from someplace and they lead to someplace.

Racism and sexism are complex social phenomena. On the one hand, they express themselves in institutional conditions, some of which are easy to detect, and on the other hand they impact on every individual in one form or another. All of the institutional forms of racism and sexism are manifest in the individuals in this country; we must stop being shocked when our comrades, our potential fighting partners, exhibit manifestations of race, sex and class bias.

Is Lesbianism a culture? This question asked at the symposium is as yet unanswered, but remains on the drawing board and is bound to the notion that because we are women "we are all equal," regardless of sexual orientation, class and colour. We need to pare the question down to a thinkable form. Is homophobia a cultural phenomenon? By the back door, the question looks easier to deal with. Sexism is the mother of homophobia. Males who prefer males pay dearly for refusing to participate in the macho culture of the majority of men in this country. Women who prefer women pay dearly because they insist upon living outside the realm of sexist victimization. It is all so much misogyny.

Sexism is definitely cultural. It defines how people in this society relate to one another. Who is in control and who is not; how things are done and how they are not done. It determines what we talk about and how we say the things we say; it even defines what we are silent about. Most important, sexism defines our emotions. What we see and don't see, hear and don't hear, feel and don't feel are all defined by the culture from which we arise.

Racism is layered between the sexism of this society and is connected to sexism. So intimately bound are they that sometimes their separation leads to confusion in the minds and hearts of women, even fear. The condition of white privilege delineates the nature of the cultural resistance of women of colour and demarcates the lines of authority, the hierarchy between women. Lesbians are "expected to pass," but only white lesbians can actually do so. Although coloured lesbians may appear heterosexual, they cannot move outside their skin. As such, although racism is new and sexism is old, it is racism that shapes the condition of women.

To experiment with ideological questions as they affect the personal is a privilege in North America, a white-skinned privilege, not extended to a minority of poor, white single mothers. Those of us women of colour who have achieved the class privilege that ordinary citizens enjoy are acutely aware that the majority of our people do not live this way. To object to racism or sexism without challenging oneself, whether we are white or coloured, is to deny privilege. All those with privilege are expected to "pass." Many of us accept the privilege without challenge.

All of the writers in this book are women who are struggling to object; struggling to remain cognizant that we wish to represent not the elite we have risen to or been born to, but those whose condition demands our attention. We strive to represent the elimination of all forms of suffering without being condescending. We don't always succeed; our lack of success has made us suspicious of each other at times. We understand that trust is a social question, a historical one, not an ahistorical one. We understand that trust between women of colour and white women requires that white women take on racism, fight it at every opportunity as though they truly believed that this fight was in their own interest because it is. Just as we understand that trust between men and women will come only when men take on anti-sexist struggles, whether or not we are there urging them to do so. We also know that until choice around sexual orientation exists for women, all of our choices will be limited.

Our response to racism, sexism and homophobia is going to be a cultural response, first because we are writers, cultural workers, and second because the phenomena are expressed culturally in the world we live in. If the culture in which we live cannot accommodate new thoughts, new feelings, new relationships, then we need a *cultural revolution*. As writers, cultural workers, we take this on.

Sky Lee

Yelling It: Women and Anger Across Cultures[1]

To begin with, as I sit down to write this article, I try to imagine who would read it. I decide I would like to imagine you as nice white feminist-idealists waiting for me to tell all. I scan your leisurely faces, row on row like daisies. Nice, receptive, encouraging expressions—well fed but still hungry for something. I don't know what.

I feel reticent about what I need to say, not only because I haven't written an essay in years, but also because I myself am never satisfied with half-truths, so why should I think that any of you would be?

There are many ways to broach the subject of being a writer-participant in this conference, and the idea(l)s which that stirs in me, but so many things get in the way. Things like racism, homophobia, misogyny; all those dirty-minded schisms occupy my mind instead. Why do I feel like I have to explain them at all? As if I cannot rest easy until I at least include those words somewhere in my ten-page editorial. I guess it is because I am a woman of colour (meaning of course, that I am a colourful woman). And maybe that circumstance is supposed to make me gasp and ooh and aah, and exclaim, "Well then, that makes me very special, doesn't it, dear? Why else would I be trying so hard to explain myself?" And here I go again, feeding those pompous, pious ideas that we all have roles to play, positions to take, and opinions to state.

Do you know what I'd really like to do instead?

Most of all, what I really want to do is sidle up to you, and feel your arms, how strong your shoulders, look into your mouth, marvel at your eyelashes. And I want you to smile at me, run your fingers through my hair, and marvel at my navel. Before long, I probably would venture out, because I do want to tell you what my idea(l)s are. Really, I do. Here, I'll even begin. I would say,

"Culture is fluid, you know."

And you would know, because our communication would be a clear example of that fluidity. You watch my lips, and I read your gaze. I feel the warmth of your heart, and you touch the breath of my soul. Ooh, look how simple, how easy the exchange after all!

Now if only this "pain of glass" weren't in the way. It is glass, isn't it? It feels cold, impenetrable, smooth, hard. I can see you, but I can't feel you. When I reach out for the feel of another human being, I hit a barrier which is sometimes invisible, sometimes just hard to describe. Its density is impossible to gauge, because when I first encountered it (about ten lifetimes ago), I was very young, had no tools with which to measure it and no language with which to describe it. By now, I have a fairly accurate and intuitive way of comparing its various forms and thicknesses, but still haven't any reference points in common with you in order to measure it for you, and hence prove to you that it even exists.

I probably wouldn't prove it to you anyways. I just know that there are many things which can't be boxed and slotted and labelled, not even when the order of the good ol' boys absolutely demands it. And many of you are still very much attached to the order of the good ol' boys because it is all you know, and besides, if you conform to its definitions of womanhood (or manhood, for that matter)—that is, a fashionable skin colour, staying perpetually youthful (dumb) and in awe of its principles—then it is safe enough. To you, I do not waste my words. Because the pain is so thick, you are unable to hear or sense, not if I scream myself hoarse. Not even when millions of the brown ones of us, the female ones of us, the black, white, children ones of us die like flies, would you see.

However, there are a few of you pressed up to the thinner sections of glass, trying to reach out to me. You press with all your might to get my attention; you bang your fists, get your noses out of joint. Your voices are muffled and garbled by the pain. I get sucked into banging my head against the wall too. I want you to know that it is an understanding of powerlessness which is the source of my power but my voice is dreamlike, vague, faraway. I get frustrated because in spite of my efforts, I still cannot reach you.

"Isn't it funny how they are not all white people on the other side," remarks an asian woman by my side. She makes me step back and stare at the whole picture in a different way.

"See there. An indian one. And there, an asian. Look, another asian way back there." She steps in close beside me, one hand on my shoulder, her head pressed against mine, so that when she points, I can easily follow her gaze.

"Oh yeah," I say, "I do see that now. Strange, I never realized that before."

"You need to look at the pain of glass which holds you hostage as well."

I look at her. And I see the child in her, who is very funny, and she makes me want to play with her. Then, I see the old hag in her. She makes me angry because she is petty and claws like an enraged cat. Sometimes, she is indulgent from another lifetime. In this life, she toils.

"Well then, how come I can see and feel and smell and hear you so clearly? You have pain too, but your kind of pain is not a barrier. I feel its softness, and rawness."

She faces me to consider the question. "I don't know. Maybe it's because we're both survivors," she offers. "I recognize you too. You are so old, you are ancient, and very, very ugly. And you are a very powerful crone."

I have a vague understanding of her meaning, but I cannot rationalize it. But, by now, I know I don't have to rationalize it. By now, I am compelled by what we have discovered together. I feel safe, protected, unafraid; I know something that others do not. The next step is inevitable, is to test our limitations, of course.

Lo and behold, alongside of me stands an indigenous woman. I say to her, "The only place you can find beauty anymore is where its oppressors have overlooked it." (Milan Kundera)

She says, "I finally figured you out. You're crazy. You're beautiful but you're crazy. Hey, do you want to go down to the beach? It's such a beautiful day. There is a brisk wind down at the beach."

We go happily together, hand in hand. We laugh at familiar things. I tell her about the barriers between people; there are definitely none between us, I tell her. I speak to the essential in her; and she answers back. My goddess, she is still able to answer back. I am in utopia. She is beautiful, and I fall in love.

I ignore all those non-essentials, and aim straight for her heart. I think this is enough but then, of course, I begin to want more. I want her to stay by my side. I wonder why she sometimes stands so still, and looks so terrified. One day, I reach in and get slashed, not once, not twice, but many times, and pretty close to my heart too. I look up from my bleeding wounds, and then I see that she stands on shards of pain. She is pretty badly cut up too. Yes, I have been a talented girl. I can aim for her heart but once there, I discover I must stand very still like she does out of terror. Shattered glass fragments everywhere, when I try to manoeuver, when I try to pull her out. She doesn't want to leave. This is her limitation; what she is used to.

When I wail at the top of my lungs, riight into her ear, she can hear every pitch, and gets quite drenched by my pool of tears, but she does/can/will not move an inch. Finally, I am cried out. I snuffle out loud, "But this is worse. This is worse. This is more hurtful."

She would have been better off with the pain of glass thick and intact. She would not miss what she is not aware of. And then at least, she would have been able to function. What is the use? The barriers are so powerful, so intricate, so internalized. Where do we begin? What is the sense? More attempts will just bring more anguish into her large dark eyes, so much like mine. I am torn. I feel defeated.

This is as far as I have gotten in my search, in my journey, in my life. So, what were you expecting! Nice neat theories and solutions? Pretty words of encouragement? The tried and true recipe to unlearn racism? How to ignore the urban emptiness and pretend we haven't made great cultural deserts out of our mother earth books?

Can I ask you another question? Have you ever walked down the street, believing you are a free woman, to encounter an older woman whose eyes are as blank as glass, and she can't see you, because her whole being is concentrating on how to stay upright in her high-heeled shoes which she volunteers on herself every day. Does something like that scare the shit out of you? Can I tell you that it "putrefies" me? I can still remember what women were like in ancient times, and to compare that with what I see today is too depressing. There are days upon days when I can't even bring myself to leave my apartment. I must live with this oppressive sadness every day of my life. It warps my mind. When nice people come to ask me about my cultural difference, I feel like telling them all right—telling them right off. I don't apologize for my anger. It's the best I can do for now. In my bleakest moments, I think about how ridiculous I look, banging my silly head senseless against these walls, remembering something now gone, wanting something more human. So, none of you look any better.

◇

I feel TELLING IT: WOMEN AND LANGUAGE ACROSS CULTURES, as a showcase for native-asian-lesbian women writers was very gratifying. Of course, the conference made some dreadful assumptions, for example, the format did nothing to challenge the status quo, but considering what I live with every day out there on the streets, I can probably live with those. However, if the conference's hidden agenda asked for conformity to or concurrence with feminist mores or ideals from the women involved, then IT DIDN'T GET IT!

Here is a quote from Sarah L. Hoagland's *Lesbian Ethics: Toward New Value*:

> One white lesbian academic administrator develops and produces a women of colour series. At a surface level, the basis of her decision is reasonable, even valid... Two other white lesbians write a grant to fund a conference and then invite women of colour to participate. From the perspective of these directors, they are creating opportunities, where there were none before, for women of diverse backgrounds—they are being politically responsible... doing grunt work: handling the organizational details so that

> others may have the opportunity to communicate, interact, learn. . . . from the perspective of those on whose behalf they act, they are simply representatives of the white. . . (power) structure. They may offer goodies, and they may be sufficiently manipulable. . . to provide everything demanded, but they are still in control. . . [2]

I interpret Hoagland's message to be that due to our internalized patriarchal values, one group will inevitably be seen as being paternalistic, which of course prevents the other group from seeing themselves as peers. Unless these values are confronted, then even the most altruistic intentions of such meetings and conferences become distortions which ultimately accomplish no more than the reaffirmation of male power structures.

What is feminism except anti-anti-feminism (A. Dworkin), anti-feminism being the predominant human standard on the planet today. Here again feminists feed the patriarchy by narrowly focussing their energies in a vain attempt to counter it. Is this what leads many to say that feminism is the last bastion of patriarchy? A more realistic option might be to widen the perspective on ourselves in all our diversity. However, given that "pain of glass" barrier, how many of us really have the guts?

At the TELLING IT conference, those women who did follow the prescribed mode of feminist social behaviour were not allowed to be "racist." In fact, plenty of deference was given to women of diverse cultures, perhaps as a social veneer to cover up the paucity of real cross-cultural understanding. One woman of colour was defiant enough to say that in her view, the presence of lesbians at this conference discriminated against women writers of different cultures. In effect, she was saying that there was no place for lesbians at this conference. There was a shocked silence, then a polite recovery, but incredibly, no anger. Silence can be a most effective form of rejection, especially from a superior to a subordinate, however in this case, I do feel the lack of response-ability was because she was a woman of colour, supposedly speaking from her culture, and no one wanted to risk being "racist." Certainly, I didn't, and certainly, I was angry, then confused that I along with many others had not an outlet for our anger. And again, the pain of glass thickens.

Audre Lorde said it isn't the anger that kills; it is the silence. Anger, although not independent of reasoning, comes straight from the heart, and of course, it is the first thing we silence. Without outlet it turns easily into separatist fear, which is trickier but still uncontainable. It will come out to spite the best and the phoniest of intentions. Audre also said that if that anger can be focused with precision, it can bring about racial change:

> Anger is the grief of distortions between peers, and its object is change . . . It implies peers meeting upon a common basis to examine difference, and to alter those distortions which history has created around difference.[3]

The keyword here is of course "peers"—it was not a conference of peers, and this clearly needs re-evaluating. But can we muster our courage to face this anger and hate within all of us? Can we muster our courage to face women of colour's anger? Can we muster our courage to face white women's hate? And do we have the purity of heart (and I certainly don't mean the boys' club definition of purity of heart) to purge the toxins in all of us? I wish that if we as women of conscience can claim anything at all, it would be that we have the intelligence to aim straight from our hearts.

Let's risk ourselves. Joanne Arnott, a writer to watch out for, suggested that we do a conference called YELLING IT: WOMEN AND ANGER ACROSS CULTURES. I am fascinated by the idea, but for the longest time couldn't figure out a workshop technique to express anger safely. By now, I know we can't express anger safely. We all face a terrible, burning rage. And we probably will get burnt—some just sunburnt, some badly blistered—but we do need to go through the purge. However, in a workshop, there could be lots of support as we attend each other through the hurt. There could be lots of womanly hands to gently apply cooling salve when we want. I once listened to a theory that racial hatred is actually a form of mental illness. Then there is the concept that hate is really wounded love. Do we have the guts to find out? As a nurse (crone), I can't guarantee it, but I bet in any case, we will all recover, and feel better about ourselves.

As a writer, I have learned to take risks. It feels like this: All around is darkness. I can't see a thing. But I know I've stepped off the edge of the cliff about fifteen steps back, and am standing in mid-air. Well, I've come this far; I decide to risk another step. And as I do, again, a hand comes up at that precise moment to support my foot. Scary shit or what!

Last but not least, I'm going to go back to my friend, and I'm going to yell at her. It may not be nice; I don't know if it's the right thing to do. But I am pissed off at her, and it's the best I can do for now. I will/do/can not give up that easily. For sure, I'll watch out for those sharp, shattered shards. I'll probably get tired of screaming at her; I may get close enough to touch her again. I don't know what will happen. I guess I have faith that something will happen.

Sources

1. Title by Joanne Arnott.
2. Sarah Lucia Hoagland, *Lesbian Ethics: Toward New Value* (Palo Alto, CA: Institute of Lesbian Studies, 1988).
3. Audre Lorde, "The Uses of Anger," *Women's Studies Quarterly* 9, No. 3 (Fall 1981). Reprinted in *Sister Outsider*.

Sky Lee: Afterword

I remember that the experience at the TELLING IT conference was a very rich one for me; I came with my woman of colour context and felt very much at home there. At the time, I was searching for a larger context, but only half-heartedly. I had not found anything which caught my eye, and the insecurities of venturing into the unknown were too prohibitive. I guess I over-stayed my old context.

Trust my good friend Jamila Ismail to come and jolt me out of it. She had read the unedited transcripts of the conference, and got quite excited about them. She thought they were fascinating and very readable, and so much happened at this conference that she wished that she had been there.

"You know," she said, "As I read through the proceedings, I really felt one woman's isolation. If I were her, I would have backed out too."

I was shaken, because Jamila reminded me that I should have recognized that isolation better than I did. There was a time when I was very isolated too—say when my command of English was not up to snuff, not high functioning enough for the race. Those were times when I felt horribly inadequate in facing this racial oppression, as every new immigrant, old immigrant, rooted indigenous or ungrounded indigenous has been made to feel inadequate, and isolated. I have not a specific formula for overcoming this hurt. Lots of soul-searching perhaps; caring, intelligent friends on the same quest maybe. However, I think that one knows when one has finally "licked it" by being able to see through and then beyond it: for example, the use of the word "race" in the English language, with all the values and ideals of competition, jealousy and hatred innate within the word. I am able to see this. I am able to take it or leave it.

Staying within my woman of colour context has helped me see clearly this tool of oppression. But staying safe within my woman of colour context does not help me get beyond it. Many women at the conference agreed that defining oneself within a specific community was very limiting. I also think that unless we do see through and then beyond these values, we all run the risk of alienating ourselves even more. I get rejected, so I learn to reject. So we all reject each other over and over again. I am not listened to, not heard, so I learn to silence and censor. Worse still, if I have come to rely on spoon-feeding by those who I believe have more command than me, then I will find myself spoon-feeding and disempowering others. We may get lost in the maze forever.

"This woman is brave," added Jamila. "She timidly, shakingly laid an offering out in front of the conference. This offering was a split."

It might as well have been a bomb. The participants responded like startled birds fluttering off a branch. Afterwards, it was a matter of where pieces of us landed. Which side of the split? Which ones landed on the in-between places? How many kept on fluttering?

What was this split? Well, as a matter of fact, many people came with many different ones: the difference was they stayed to tell us how they reconnected. As Asian-Canadian women writers, both Jamila and I heard Joy Kogawa when she talked about having to make the choice between the roles of dutiful daughter and self-centred writer. As woman writers, we risk becoming the renegade as we become more response-able to the truths we uncover about our lives as women. In the same room sat those who choose the dutiful daughter, along with those who choose the renegade; many of us choose to run the gauntlet, no matter how exhausting, back and forth between the two. Afterwards, Joy offered us her way of reconnecting, which was a spiritual, creative way, and I appreciated its gentleness.

There were many women who came to this same conference just as timidly, just as shakingly with offerings of a connection. And a conference is already a difficult enough forum upon which to lay the thin stalks of this fragile connection. Did they get the attending that they needed? Or did the energies get drained away by this woman's questions as to why white lesbians would want to connect their words and their names to Native and Asian women. Afterwards, she left, without offering any way of reconnecting. There is a gaping hole of silence in her wake because she censored both our words and her words. She left me wounded because I am a lesbian of colour.

Ironically, I have also questioned white lesbians' motives, but I like to believe that I have stayed to listen. Some tell me that they believe their lesbian context is large enough for women of colour. Like everything else, I must mull that over (assuming of course, that white lesbians are sincere, and will no longer make the mistake of tokenizing women of colour). Others were very quick to say no, it is just another unconnected context which is very different from the women of colour one. But this leads me to want to ask, "Is the women of colour context large enough for lesbians?"

With a sigh, a little discouraged because there are so few assurances, I start to make a move outside of what was once my safe realm. My biggest strength is that I came to my lesbian context via my woman of colour context. In my way of thinking, they are one. I hope there are other women who are also setting out on this quest for a bigger space which can accommodate diversity. Maybe, we will connect halfway. I sure do wish that I could offer them something for the road.

Here again I rely on my friend, Jamila Ismail. I said to her, white feminists and lesbians have at least made themselves accessible to women of colour. So why do we have this instinct to fight them? Jamila told me about a newspaper story she had read, about a woman bandit leader in India, who was quoted as saying, "For five years, we worshipped our weapons because we didn't have anything else." I have to agree with Jamila; the women of colour here are much like that too.

Betsy Warland

*Where our loyalties lie**

TELLING IT: WOMEN AND LANGUAGE ACROSS CULTURES was a conference about marginalized women writers. I was invited to speak as a lesbian writer. This meant to me that even though I am a White woman, as a lesbian, I was speaking from *within* the struggle to be heard. It seems to me that the general hatred and denial that each of us talked about during those two days was our bond and our barrier. On the margin, sometimes we recognize each other with great tenderness; sometimes we rail at one another's inability to understand the profound differences and inequalities of our particular oppressions.

When the margin disappears

When my presence was questioned during the opening panel of the conference I felt stunned and hurt. Then I felt abused by this all too familiar desire to render me invisible. This sense of abuse was heightened by its similarity to the incest dynamics that I was deep in the midst of discovering at that time. I was naive in believing that this was going to be one literary conference where I felt I belonged, where I wouldn't have to defend myself as a lesbian writer. This naiveté made me feel initially betrayed. It was only later that I felt angry.

This challenge about the inclusion of lesbian writers in the conference has provoked some intense reflection among the

---

*Author's note: Given that Whites comprise a minority of the world's population and given that as feminists we are recognizing that we need to think more globally, I want to indicate this by capitalizing the word referring to European and Caucasus racial origins, just as we tend to capitalize other racial groups. If we don't capitalize White are we not making a statement that white is the norm and every other racial group is aberrant?

four editors, who through this editing and writing process are still very much participating in the conference a year-and-a-half later. Because the woman who raised the challenge is unwilling to talk about what happened (and didn't happen), we can only fill in the blanks. Not a very reliable process. For me, this challenge raises, among other things, the question of scapegoating. Have we come to terms with this instinct within the feminist communities? Does someone still have to be on the bottom? Do we still need someone or some group to be the object of our criticisms, scrutiny and judgements? I suspect we do. I suspect that we haven't really dealt with the scapegoating instinct within us and the multitudinous ways it gets expressed within the feminist communities. And is this negativity in fact patriarchal hatred of women, displaced and internalized as self-hatred?

This commentary has been the hardest thing I have ever written. Why? Primarily because I am writing beyond my own boundaries, beyond what I've said on paper before. There are other reasons. One is the fact that I am the only White woman writing a commentary and because of racism and because of the upheaval around lesbianism I have keenly felt my words being scrutinized. Throughout the course of many drafts I have received considerable feedback and criticism from the other editors. I have rewritten and rewritten this. Have said in my private, hopeless hours that I'm not going to participate in the commentaries—yet I know I must not censor myself. As a Black activist acquaintance of mine says about the struggle for equality, "You're damned if you do and you're damned if you don't!" I encouraged myself by saying that perhaps the time has come for all of us to take more chances on the page—that we need to move beyond our private conversations or formal, well-thought-out positions. But do we have the guts to risk speaking our half-formed understandings and raw emotions? Do we have the generosity to listen and question?

As the question of racism within the literary community has raged over the past couple of years, I have been frightened by the vitriolic, indignant comments and actions of White writers and publishers. I have experienced more violent anger at my anti-racist stands (in conversations and in letters and articles I've written) than I have at my lesbianism. This has often made me feel quite isolated. I do not belong to an oppressed race which is passionately working to eradicate racism. I am part of the feminist, lesbian and literary communities which are still largely White and which are still in the early stages of guilt-anger-denial-fear when it comes to racism. There are a growing number of White feminists with whom I do feel some companionship, but most of them tend to be very reluctant to make their private perceptions public. My friend Gay Alison suggests that listening is the most important thing we can do. Open ears inevitably do create open hearts. Yet if, when our hearts are beating with our most deeply held words, we are afraid to speak, nothing really changes.

Body to body, mouth to mouth

The culture that sustains and nourishes me most is the lesbian culture. Without it I would quite literally die. The lesbian culture is the only culture where my intimate life and centre (from which I experience the world) are not called into question; are not met with hatred and fear. Yet, in the public realm my culture is unarticulated and inarticulate.

We are an old culture but not an ancient culture. Ancient in the sense of a culture which at one time or another enjoyed or enjoys the powers of being the norm. We are a woman-defined culture. Consequently, we have never shaped public reality because in most cultures this control has largely been in the hands of men. Our culture has been passed on from body to body, mouth to mouth. Perhaps we are anarchic by nature.

For the most part we question and resist the "given" roles.

As Nicole Brossard says, we make ourselves up as we go along. Our culture has located itself intensely within our intimate relationships and we lack a public language. I can't help but wonder, if we do develop a public language, will other cultures be able to read a culture that hasn't been defined by the familiar codes of men? Will our public language even be legible to them? Because our lesbian culture has only been able to thrive in the intimate (the domestic), it may have a built-in resistance to the public. I suspect that the only way we will be able to create a public language will be by changing, re-forming the very concept of what the public is.

I don't think that I've ever been as acutely aware of this lack of a public language and context as I was during the conference and have been during the process of creating this book. This has made me often feel very angry and alone. The lesbian culture has no history no sacred objects no land. The art of earlier lesbians has mostly been erased either by the mainstream (which obscures the artist's lesbian identity or ignores the work) or sometimes by ourselves. Yes, we destroy or alter our own work for fear of reprisals: loss of our children, rejection by our non-lesbian friends, abandonment by our families, loss of our economic security or loss of our very lives.

Speaking her name

What I often see in feminist communities is a dangerous lack of naming our loyalties and a reluctance to honour them when things get tense. As women, we have been brainwashed to smile and keep the peace at all costs. Or, when threatened by our different loyalties, we revert back to patriarchal monovision. It happens when a friend, who is a Woman of Colour and who knows your commitment to anti-racist work, suddenly lumps you together with all White people when talking to other Women of Colour. It happens when a lesbian puts down a heterosexual friend when they are in the company of lesbians by saying "Come on, Mary—when are *you* going to 'come out'?"

It happens when a White feminist is reluctant to call another White feminist on a racist statement because she's afraid of being accused of being "holier than thou." I know that as White women it is not acceptable for us to "break ranks." That our trust is too often based on silence and behind-the-back, "private" conversations.

I'm relieved to say that a number of women spoke up during that first panel in support of lesbian writers' presence at the conference. No doubt each of them took a risk in offering her support and affirmation. Lee Maracle and I have exchanged our perceptions and feelings about how painful this can be when we take the risk of supporting someone outside our own culture. Lee gave her support of lesbian writers' participation in the conference during that first panel/audience discussion and it meant a lot to me.

I wonder if we need to explore the possibility of a new kind of commitment which doesn't rely on sameness or the feminist façade of solidarity or individual solutions?

As White women, I know that when *we own our individual oppression and/or abuse*, we are dislocated from our illusory place in the status quo. It is within the outlawed communities of active feminists, lesbians, incest survivors, differently-abled, single mothers, goddess worshipers, etc., that we can begin to find the resources we need for throwing off our oppression. It is here, on the margin, that we can also experience a growing awareness of the necessity to refuse our former complicity with other forms of patriarchal oppressions which differ from our own.

A gentle circling

One of the ways of being I so appreciated during the conference was the Native writers' emphasis on the importance of listening. Because of this, the participating writers and the women attending the conference often listened and spoke with more care than I've experienced at other conferences. Women frequently were deeply moved by what other women said. Tears were part of this listening. Although we have edited most of it out (because of space considerations and because it seemed too formal on the page), women often publicly thanked the previous speaker for what she had said on the panel or during the panel/audience discussion or during the workshops.

When a speaker brought up a controversial issue, she wasn't attacked. A gentle circling occurred whereby the discussion would move on to another topic, then circle back to the controversial statement, then go on and then circle back again. Each circling back seemed to bring at least the beginnings of a greater clarity, a greater honesty. But as much as I appreciated this, I don't wish to idealize the conference. There still were numerous comments and questions (publicly and privately stated) that were ignorantly racist. Although the conference approach to listening and speaking was an improvement, we have a long way to go in figuring out how to more immediately and directly confront and name our racist, homophobic and classist behaviours.

I do think that many of the women attending and participating in the conference began to speak their differences in perception more publicly. One of the most moving exchanges in which it was very evident that our differences don't cancel out the truth of our words was when Joy Kogawa revealed her painfully gained insight as to how she too could oppress others. Yet this insight was not reflective of the vision of Lee Maracle, who vividly reminded us that her people's history and present day circumstance are very different.

Is lesbian a culture?

What does it mean when the use of the term "lesbian writer" is considered to be unnecessary and divisive? The

Woman of Colour who disputed my participation suggested that lesbianism isn't a culture because lesbians don't have a language and, in her experience, the literature of a culture is identified by its language. Was the conference creating discrimination and divisiveness by labeling a woman as a "lesbian writer?"

For me, the answer to that question is no. And yet the woman who questioned my presence at the conference speaks in fact for most people. It never ceases to amaze me when heterosexuals accuse lesbians or gays of being divisive and discriminatory when we are visible, while we must live with the wholesale promoting of heterosexual images and attitudes and values every day. Let's get it clear here *who* is doing the discriminating, whose laws and whose violence is being turned *on who* so routinely that most heterosexuals rarely even think about it. Just what are English Canadian women writers (who are feminists) saying when they are calling lesbian-content writing "exclusive," "prescriptive," "divisive," "limited," "naive," "binary" and "based on simple solutions." Let me tell you if there's one thing that lesbianism is not Is simple! Thank the goddess that it brings so much joy along with the pain.

Is lesbianism not a culture because we don't have our own language? There are, in fact, many cultures which don't appear to have their own language. In some of these cultures the original language has been "lost," which means it has been destroyed by another invading and colonizing culture. And there are cultures which, for example, seem to speak the same language (such as English), yet true communication is very difficult and rarely occurs. Lesbian culture certainly has elements which suggest our own language: we have phrases, code-words, reclaimed words which are specific to us.

There are lesbian writers, such as Gertrude Stein, whose codes for lesbian intimacy and eroticism we are still attempting to decipher. Stein's writing is a continuing source of fascination and delight because of her coding. It is also a source of sadness and loss. She is one of my culture's mothers and like so many other of our mothers, she stands so unrevealed to most of us. And, although there have been some gains made in the publishing, distribution and reception of explicit lesbian writing, the grid of the code is still very much in place. It can be slightly intoxicating to learn the language and the code as a new member of the lesbian community. For most of us, we have always felt we didn't fit, were different, were somehow outsiders, and access to a coded language that names our difference, in our own terms, is very affirming. Yet, it is also a symbol of our oppression. This is why in the first book I wrote as a lesbian (*open is broken*), I felt compelled to break open the code and reclaim a lesbian erotic language which was more public and accessible.

A significant part of our language is expressed nonverbally. Body language (how we walk, sit, take up public space, how our voice comes from our centre of gravity) and clothes comprise our most crucial forms of intra-cultural communication. This is the only way we can recognize each other beyond our circle of friends and political activities. Although I've often heard heterosexuals insist that they can spot a lesbian a mile off, heterosexual women and men, in fact, have no concept of the subtlety, rapidity or complexity of this "language." A language which is absolutely crucial to our survival and sense of connection in the public world.

As a lesbian, I am a woman who belongs to no man. This simple fact creates a dramatic shift in how I perceive the world (and how the world perceives me!). Lesbian women relinquish the protection of men. And in a world that is so systematically and arbitrarily distrustful of and violent to women, this is serious business. It means that as lesbians, we are responsible for ourselves in every way: economically, socially, spiritually, etc. Many of us who have lived in committed couple relationships for years still function autonomously when it comes to money. Most of us must give up the hope and notion that "someone is going to take care of us." We realize the price that is paid for that reliance.

I've known a lot of strong lesbian and heterosexual feminists over the years and I have watched how this hope and notion is one of the most difficult things to give up. It appears in many disguises. It is deeply ingrained in our socialization and I believe it is one of the most destructive aspects of our relationships to men. The very structure of the economy and the patriarchal nuclear family conspires to keep us afraid and dependent. We are fortunate if as lesbians we can maintain an honest and accepting relationship with our blood families. Usually it is with only a member or two. So, we make our own non-blood, chosen families to whom our commitments run very deep.

With this self-reliance comes the right to create who we are. We are not having to continually explain and negotiate this right with a male intimate. We *must* make ourselves and this making is the source of much of our pleasure and vision. Everything is renewed in its process.

After the experience of the conference, I also believe that the feminist communities have not honestly confronted their homophobia. Heterosexual feminists need to really listen to the stories of our invisible lesbian culture; they need to understand that the differences between lesbians and themselves are far greater than how we make love.

Erasure from within and without

In Marlene Wildeman's essay "Theorizing Lesbian Existence" [*Fireweed*, Summer 1989], she writes, "Is it really a form of treason to ask to what extent we [lesbians] can expect heterosexual feminists to struggle for goals specific to lesbians?" As lesbians, we often comprise much of the backbone for the work being done in the women's movement. Even though a significant amount of this work has been for the benefit of heterosexual women, our heterosexual sister-workers, as Wildeman reminds, have often asked us to hide our lesbianism from the public, from the funders and from other heterosexual women. In essence, we lesbians have all too often agreed to erase ourselves in the interests of our heterosexual sisters. I very much believe that this is one of the reasons we are accused of being divisive when we finally name ourselves. We're supposed to "pass."

Lesbian culture is often incorporated into or presented as "feminist culture" and "women's culture." Again, we often agree to be represented by these larger, "more inclusive" terms for the "larger" cause, yet this inclusiveness erases us. An American friend of mine, Lise Weil, who was offering a university course called "Lesbian Literature," was forced to drop "lesbian" from the course title after numerous students who wanted to take the course (many of whom were lesbians) came to her and told her that they couldn't take the course because they couldn't have "that word" on their transcripts.

As lesbians we are fortunate because most of us can pass for heterosexual if need be, or at least we can take an occasional break from the relentlessness of our oppression. Women of Colour do not have this option. But are we "more fortunate" or is this very option of passing part and parcel of society's strategy for eradicating us? Is not the hatred and fear of lesbians so profound as to deny our very existence? In most countries, laws about homosexuality only refer to men. As Barbara Herringer recently said to me, "Can you imagine a bill being debated in Parliament about lesbians?" Can you imagine federal funding ever being given for an explicitly lesbian writers' conference or school or publication?

Although our music, art, sport and political activities tend to be a little more visible, the domestic, social, health, ethical, erotic, intellectual and spiritual aspects of our lives are still quite private and invisible. Barbara Herringer pointed out during the second panel discussion that as lesbians we "haven't even begun" to publicly articulate our culture.

Good-bye to one dame one name

I would suggest that we must have the right to use all our names. No one name can say who we are. Otherwise we get stuck in such conundrums as "Lesbian doesn't mean Woman of Colour; Woman of Colour doesn't mean lesbian." Sometimes it is cumbersome but if we give in to the patriarchal insistence on circling the correct answer (as if there were multiple choices—more than one right answer), we are once again in danger of serious erasure.

Many women embody more than one loyalty. When, say, you are a Black lesbian incest survivor, you are forced to seek out various communities to meet your needs. These different communities may not only have little to do with each other, they may even be hostile towards one another. I wonder if these women aren't our transformers. For these feminists, embracing difference isn't an ideology but a day-to-day necessity. And it is in their learning to make peace with themselves and others that they transform our mono-loyalties and open up the possibilities of support beyond "our own." For many of us, our multi-loyalties may not be as apparent but the same transforming capacity also applies.

Cross-loyalties

If we are really committed to building a multi-racial feminist community, we need to stop saying things like "It's a shame more Women of Colour didn't attend the conference." We have to learn new ways of organizing our gatherings and sharing the decision-making process so that our White structures (of mind & of site) no longer dominate. If we say we believe that feminism is much larger than our own particular life's circumstance and vision, then we need to think what we're doing when we dismiss another woman who sees things differently with statements like "She's not really a feminist." We'd probably gain a lot by refraining from that dismissal. We'd probably learn a lot more by listening to her, speaking only when, as Sky Lee says, we can "aim straight from our hearts."

I like the statement which Joy Kogawa made (*see* PANEL TWO, *Audience Discussion*) ". . . I think it's important to be able to move out of one identity into another and to look for the core of why it is that you would choose to be any single identity." Audre Lorde names herself as "Black feminist lesbian warrior poet." Gloria Anzaldúa writes in *Borderlands/La Frontera* [spinsters/aunt lute, 1987] about being a lesbian and a feminist and coming from a multi-racial heritage. Here she speaks of her multi-cultural cross-loyalties:

> To live in the Borderlands means you
> are neither *hispana india negra española*
> *ni gabacha, eres mestiza, mulata,* half-breed
> caught in the crossfire between camps
> while carrying all five races on your back
> not knowing which side to turn to, run from . . .
>
> To survive the Borderlands means
> you must live *sin fronteras*
> be a crossroads.

As women, we focus much of our energy on relationships and we tend to be multi-relational. Although this feminine quality has been considered a weakness by the patriarchy, at this point in the story of the world I believe this way of being and seeing is very necessary. To honour one of our loyalties does not mean that we must deny or betray our other loyalties. Our hearts know the call of many names.

Biographical Notes

JEANNETTE ARMSTRONG is an Okanagan Indian writer and educator from Penticton, British Columbia, who has published two books for children, *Enwhisteekwa* (*Walk In Water*) and *Neekna and Chemai*, and a novel, *Slash*. She is currently director and co-founder of the En'owkin International School of Writing in Penticton.

BARBARA HERRINGER is a writer, editor and social worker presently living in Victoria, B.C. Her work has appeared in various journals over the last few years, including *Fireweed*, *Room of One's Own*, *Sinister Wisdom*, *West Coast Review*, *Kinesis*, *The Radical Reviewer*, *CV II*, and in the book *Lesbian Nuns: Breaking Silence*. In the early 1980s she co-founded and edited the journal *The Radical Reviewer*; since 1989 she has been on the advisory committee of *(f.)Lip*, a journal of feminist innovative writing. She was involved at the outset in creating the Women and Words Conference and Society, and was a member of the editorial group for *Women and Words: The Anthology*. She is currently working on a suite of poems and co-editing/writing a book on feminist social work practice in Canada.

JOY KOGAWA is a Japanese-Canadian living in Toronto, Ontario, best known for her novel *Obasan* about the internment of the Japanese during World War II. She has also published several volumes of poetry, most recently *Women in the Woods* (1985). Her writings reflect and focus on her oriental background and she has been actively involved in the Japanese-Canadian redress issue. She is currently writing a sequel to *Obasan*.

SKY LEE, born thirty-eight years ago in Alberni, B.C., currently lives in Vancouver where she earns wages as a nurse, mothers a six-year-old, loves a good woman, writes short stories and takes flying leaps in life. Her short stories have been published in *Vancouver Short Stories*, edited by Carole Gerson (U.B.C. Press: 1985), and in the journals *West Coast Review*, *Asianadian* and *Time Capsule*. Her illustrations have appeared in *Teach Me How to Fly, Skyfighter*, by Paul Yee, in the anthology *Inalienable Rice* and in *Makara* magazine and *May Day* magazine. Her novel, *Disappearing Moon Cafe*, was published by Douglas and McIntyre in spring 1990.

LEE MARACLE is the author of two books, *Bobbi Lee: Indian Rebel* and *I Am Woman*, published by The Women's Press (Toronto: 1990) and Write-On Press (North Vancouver: 1988), respectively. She has published a number of articles in magazines and newsletters, and has collaborated on numerous poetry/music tapes with other Native poets and Black poets in Canada. She is currently a full-time student at Simon Fraser University and is working on a collection of short stories and two books of poetry to be published in the next year by Press Gang Publishers (Vancouver) and Write-On Press (North Vancouver). As well, several pieces of her non-fiction have been published or are slated for publication in anthologies. *Frictions*, an anthology of women's stories published by Second Story Press (Toronto: 1989) includes a story written by her son and herself. Between all that, Lee travels, reads poetry and tries to keep her children fed and on-track.

DAPHNE MARLATT is the author of numerous books of poetry and/or prose, including *Steveston*, *Touch to my Tongue* and *How Hug a Stone*. Her most recent publications are a novel, *Ana Historic*, and a poetic collaboration with Betsy Warland, *Double Negative*. She has edited or co-edited several little magazines, two oral histories and *in the feminine: women and words/les femmes et les mots conference proceedings 1983*. Currently, she continues co-editing *Tessera*, a journal of new Québécoise and English-Canadian feminist theory and writing, and she is working on her next book of poetry, *Salvage*.

LOUISE PROFEIT–LEBLANC is a northern Tutchone woman. Born and raised in the Yukon, she grew up in an environment conducive to Native storytelling, an art practised for thousands of years by her people as a method of healing. Louise has broken tradition by reading her people's legends over radio, and she is excited about being one of those who is taking oral history and developing it into a written format for future generations. She has taken legends and turned them into poems and recently she has gone one step further by developing and narrating a video, *Star Sisters*, which portrays a legend through animation. Her position as Native Heritage Advisor to the Yukon government has provided her with an opportunity to liaise with all of the Native communities of the Yukon to assist them in protecting their heritage culturally and artistically.

VANCOUVER SATH, formed in early 1983, is a collective of Punjabi writers and artists from the lower mainland of British Columbia. Among Sath's objectives are to consciously create and promote theatre and literature about the Indo-Canadian community. Since its inception Sath has produced ten plays in Punjabi and three plays in English, dealing with issues such as racism, farmworkers, violence against women, arranged marriages and religion in politics. Sath is a traditional name for a place in the Punjabi village where villagers gather and talk about contemporary issues in a very informal manner. Now in Canada, Sath is no longer a specific place but an idea which inspires their collective action. Sath includes young and old, men and women, first generation immigrants and second generation Canadian born youngsters and adults. Sath members Harjinder Sangra, Jagdish Binning, Anju Hundal and Pindy Gill have not only performed but have taken a very active part in the production and presentation of Sath's plays.

BETSY WARLAND's books of poetry include *A Gathering Instinct*, *open is broken*, and *serpent (w)rite*, as well as *Double Negative* (written in collaboration with Daphne Marlatt). Her collection of essays, articles and short prose texts, *Proper Deafinitions*, was published by Press Gang Publishers in spring 1990. She has also co-edited *in the feminine: women and words/les femmes et les mots conference proceedings 1983* and *(f.)Lip*, a newsletter of feminist innovative writing. She is currently working on an operatic play and editing a collection of essays by Canadian, Québec and U.S. lesbian writers.

Acknowledgements

Thanks to the following agencies and individuals who contributed to the conference and to the making of this book:

The Women's Studies Program, Simon Fraser University, in particular Nikki Strong-Boag, for support and for funding;

Sandy Shreve, Women's Studies Program Assistant, for co-organizing the conference with infinite care and tact—it couldn't have happened without her;

The Leon and Thea Koerner Foundation, Secretary of State/ Multiculturalism, the B.C. Women's Secretariat and The Canada Council Readings Program for funding the conference;

Viola Thomas for moderating the panel discussions;

Dave Gronley and Jergan Berwald for audio-taping all sessions;

Jill Stainsby for keeping track of speakers during audience discussions and workshops;

Evelyn Fingarson and Holly Devor for making a photographic record of the conference;

Susan MacFarlane and Sharon Oliver for transcribing many hours of tapes;

Katrina Dennis for keying in the manuscript;

The Publications Committee, Simon Fraser University, for funding for transcription;

The Explorations Program of The Canada Council for a grant to edit this book;

Press Gang Publishers, especially Barbara Kuhne, for patience and faith.

PRESS GANG PUBLISHERS FEMINIST CO-OPERATIVE is committed to publishing a wide range of writing by women which explores themes of personal and political struggles for equality.

A free listing of our books is available from Press Gang Publishers, 603 Powell Street, Vancouver, B.C. V6A 1H2 Canada